THE OLD SHOES

(THE SOUL OF AN ARTIST)

SHEWEIA

BALBOA.
PRESS

A DIVISION OF HAY HOUSE

Balboa Press books may be ordered through booksellers or by contacting:

Balboa Press
A Division of Hay House
1663 Liberty Drive
Bloomington, IN 47403
www.balboapress.com
1 (877) 407-4847

Because of the dynamic nature of the Internet, any web addresses or links contained in this book may have changed since publication and may no longer be valid. The views expressed in this work are solely those of the author and do not necessarily reflect the views of the publisher, and the publisher hereby disclaims any responsibility for them.

The author of this book does not dispense medical advice or prescribe the use of any technique as a form of treatment for physical, emotional, or medical problems without the advice of a physician, either directly or indirectly. The intent of the author is only to offer information of a general nature to help you in your quest for emotional and spiritual well-being. In the event you use any of the information in this book for yourself, which is your constitutional right, the author and the publisher assume no responsibility for your actions.

Any people depicted in stock imagery provided by Thinkstock are models, and such images are being used for illustrative purposes only.
Certain stock imagery © Thinkstock.

Printed in the United States of America.

ISBN: 978-1-4525-2170-1 (sc)
ISBN: 978-1-4525-2171-8 (e)

Balboa Press rev. date: 09/30/2014

FOREWORD

This book is to honor, celebrate, and rejoice in all the Spirits, guides, power animals, and perhaps ancestors who gave me comfort in my terror, whispered directions in my ear, and protected me from that which would harm me. I am eternally grateful for their kindness, their patience, their steadfastness, and their love.

Special thanks go to Duanne Whitehead, who was my believing mirror, pulling me through my doubts and fears, and providing me with a "ground" from which to build.

This book is also to honor the child self who remembers the dream. In all the many times, I re-read the book, I was struck by how in some ways "juvenile" it was in its approach. And then I remembered a channel that once said that the child remembers the dream but the teenager is the one who knows how to make it come true. Perhaps the language will help young adults as well as older adults to reclaim their inner child (holder of the dream) and to carry the baton forward to see it manifest - telling their story.

Unbelievable synchronicities occurred from the first page to the last, even though years separated the entries. I was in some kind of alternate reality where everything was connected and flowed as one unified whole. As I wrote in now time, the words or sentiments were repeated in songs on the radio. Every word seemed to be "heard" and some response initiated. I seemed to live between the door opening and the door closing, often not feeding the physical body in-between these eternal spans of experience.

Earth Angels
Feet of clay like Earth Shoes
Wings of Crystal like Heaven's Gate
Trees Swaying between two Worlds
Heart Breakers, Wounds and Scars
Story Collectors, Dream Weavers
and Power Deliverers
Peace Bringers and Circle Beings
Two Worlds Collide
"I AM"

This book is dedicated to David Chethlahe Paladin,
author of
*PAINTING THE DREAM: THE VISIONARY ART OF NAVAJO PAINTER
DAVID CHETHLAHE PALADIN*

PUEBLO MANDALA

*Each bowl is spun from a woman's dream
And blest with soil from the bosom of Mother Earth,
Caressed by the soft hands of its maker,
And fired with the warmth of Sun God's gift.
I take your fragments, crushing them into sand,
And reweave them, mixing in threads of my own
dream.
Mandala of beauty that was,
Mandala of beauty that is,
Circle of living dreams,
Mix your dreams with the dreams of
Those who behold you.
In beauty complete the circle
That is life itself.*

PROLOGUE

I have a story to tell. You may not believe it. It may not be true, or it may be more true than anything you have ever read. Regardless, I invite you to read it as a parable. Look underneath and beyond the words for the truth and love that allowed them to emerge. Let me paint you a picture. Your only hope of viewing this picture is to enter the space between the door closing and the door opening, a space some call "no time." Have a wonderful journey!

Perhaps the first leg of the journey begins with the life of Vincent van Gogh, an artist who was impassioned to create art with feeling and emotion. His journey can be transplanted upon my own in many ways. So as I wrote my story, his voice magnified my own. I give you the chance to hear his tones by reading his letters in reference to my experience. They are marked by a footnote with the Volume and page numbers from two volumes of *The Complete Letters of Vincent van Gogh*. You can also find more information at www.vangoghletters.org/vg/

CHAPTER 1

The Sound Of One

She wanted to live, not create a "reason" to live.

We are all Earth Angels, touching the Earth with feet of clay and touching the Heavens with crystal wings. From both worlds come our stories of who we are and who we are yet to be.

The following takes place in a small southwestern town in the United States in the year 2000. A woman artist whose name was Mya is in her middle years facing a defining moment. This is her story.

The door closes. The cat meows. My heart breaks. The world is still again… no expectations or demands… no hope. I make my futile attempt to end the silence for a greater stillness. Of course I fail. I begin circling this silence, making senseless noises to fill the void with sounds of life, but then I recall the tree falling in the middle of the forest with no one to hear the crash. I fell, too, and I wondered if anyone heard it, and if anyone heard my grappling to rise again? Did I indeed rise, or am I still stretched motionless on the floor? I'm not sure.

I hear in my mind the countless clichés about living in the moment, about not being attached to outcome, about projections, and on and on. It doesn't matter. I'm alone again. Countless ideologies, philosophies, and dogmas flash before me, but it doesn't matter; the words end in death the moment they materialize. The reality is that I am alone in this moment and the moments to follow.

"I have my work", I say to myself. "I can go on." Another voice says, "I have purpose," and yet the words sound hollow and somewhat ridiculous in the light of my present condition.

A country pop idol comes on TV, the very one I thought was "on the edge" – very expressive of the light and dark side, but now he seems like a used car salesman, hiding the fact that the speedometer has been tampered with and the engine has some major mechanical problems. The outside looks pretty good; but what's on the inside? And then it happens. I hear the guitar twang and run up and down the scale, and I want to let loose. I want to feel again for another. The music enters my soul and body, and I want to sing my song, and I want to hear his song. Pain wakes me out of my reverie, and I realize I am alone, and the music is not for my ears but for the prospective buyers of the used car. It's an illusion. I hate myself for falling again, for hoping. How could I do that again so soon after he walked out the door. I was comfortable with the numbness, but NOW THIS? The dream was dead, and yet now I AM SEDUCED INTO PICKING UP THE OLD FILM CLIPS SCATTERED ON THE THEATER FLOOR. I feel again the pain of a tragic love story, an unbearable sadness and a yearning without end. I ASK MYSELF, "WHERE IS THE MIDDLE ROAD AND CAN MY HEART MEND?

Somewhere deep inside me, I know this feeling… of pulling back from a place so cold, turning around, retracing my steps back to the pain.

I remember the impact of reading about Van Gogh, the Dutch artist who had bouts of anguish. Suddenly his words somehow entered my consciousness… something about trying to "regain the bank" as a man entering the "water" of a suicidal attempt but finding that the water was too cold and reaching back for the bank.[1]

I retraced my steps and my stories and all their patterns until everything ended one day in one sound, the sound of a door closing, shutting. In that one moment, time stood still and demanded no stories, only truth. One small whisper of a sound echoed throughout eternity. With eyes closed, I didn't see the figure move away from me, as his spirit slipped through the closed door. I lay there frozen with grief and shock in the nothingness. My hopes and dreams were shattered; no semblance of identity or essence remained. I was just a body lying there on the bed, one foot nudged against the bedpost to keep from falling further into the abyss. There was nothing, no movement, no hope of tomorrow, or anything else.

I finally rose and became enamored with the SACRED KNIFE lying on the table. I had used it many times to "cut through" illusion in shamanic journeys and to seek truth while standing in front of my easel. I picked it up, took it out of its sheath and started peeling the paint off the blade. The knife seemed to have a will of its own, and it wanted to plunge into flesh. I told myself I wanted to end the pain, but what pain? My emotions seemed to be numbed by the total stillness. My rational mind pointed out there would be blood; it would be messy; and death would not be a surety. But the knife wanted something. It wanted directness; it wanted swift action; it wanted to cut through the body to the soul. It wanted to go home. I held the knife above my navel, and the point pricked at my skin. My will pulled it back as my hand shook violently between two opposing intentions. What was I thinking? I wasn't thinking. What was I feeling? I wasn't feeling. All that existed was the will of the knife. I really should call for help – but what was the point? This was my moment; what could anyone lend to the crisis except platitudes and social norms. I didn't know how I had gotten here, but I knew there was no past or future, and there was an urgent voice that would not be stilled.

---

1   Vol. III, p 207.

So I sat and waited. My heart pounding, I considered letting it cease beating at all, and I knew I had the power to do that. Was this insanity? If you chose to cease breathing, didn't there have to be a reason? I had none. If you chose to cease breathing, didn't you have to justify it somehow? I had no justification. All I knew was that I was "used up." The reality was that I found no release from the loneliness and the yearnings in my body - at least I couldn't find it — what kind of sick joke was this? It wasn't that I hadn't looked. My God, I had searched every nook and cranny. So I sat, closed my eyes, and let the colors swirl over my consciousness — as impersonal as waves crashing over the shore. A small thread of consciousness said, "You should call for help." It was a duty I felt, not a wish – so I called my teacher, who had taught me about shamanism. No reply. I had lost the ability to form words: so the message I left was uttered with great difficulty, and long spaces EXISTED BETWEEN the words. I had hoped that she would answer the phone and say a word, anything, that would pull me from the edge of darkness. However, I also knew there was a reason I had not reached her: some decisions must be made alone. Then I sat, called a friend, and reported my condition, saying that to end my life would be the easiest thing I had ever done and feeling shocked THAT I HAD UTTERED THESE WORDS AND THAT I BELIEVED THEY WERE TRUE. I had always thought that no matter what happened, one would have some flash or insight AT THE END TO PREVENT ENDING IT ALL. But what was I ending? I didn't know; I only knew that every fiber of my body wanted it - had to have it. All this because one door softly shut? I don't think so. It was all the doors before it that had shut. It was all the searching for love, for acceptance, for a place in the world. It was my heart breaking at the shattering of dreams, and hopes, and thwarted efforts toward anything positive. It was all the disappointments and regrouping afterwards and pulling myself up, saying, "Maybe next time. Maybe the next painting. Maybe I'll meet someone." I did believe in miracles - so why not. But I heard the sound of that door again. So impersonal, him leaving that way, walking away unfettered. So easy him closing that door - sluffing off the affair and focusing on details of ordinary life and business. So easy to walk away leaving me there. "What did it matter anyway - just a misunderstanding."

I projected myself into my lover's mind. "She thought I was available for love. The truth is I never have been. She thought she could make her love penetrate my shell. Just a misunderstanding. She thought she could touch me and I could feel her tenderness and caring beyond sex. What's the big deal? I simply went through a door - I had to attend to business. I asked her what I could do for her--but she didn't reply. What more could I do? She needed to rest anyway, so I left her. It was cumbersome because before I could leave, I had to scrape her up off the floor in front of the door. I hadn't lied – she just misunderstood."

I came back to my own state of mind after imagining his, wanting to keep hope alive. I was caught between my sexuality, my rationality, my empathy, and my spirituality. I wanted to feel, to touch, to caress. I wanted to heal the denied parts of myself. I wanted to love, to be loved. I wanted to drink and eat until I was no longer thirsty or hungry. I wanted to feel needed - to have a symbiotic relationship. I wanted to feel alive, to be part of something: a plan, a life strategy, a partnership, a meeting of minds, a common goal. I was tired of "one".

I felt Van Gogh in my soul talking about feeling "a tempest of desire to embrace something...."[2] I also felt the presence of angels nearby as if saying, "Your soul longs for more."

She wanted to respond to her passion. She wanted to be a beast, an animal, naked in the sun – pure of any defense or pretense. If this was not possible, then she didn't want anything else. The knife was the answer. It would plunge into that part of her self that needed to be touched. She was tired of processing information, tired of intellectualizing, philosophizing, creating rules by which to live. SHE WANTED TO LIVE, NOT CREATE A REASON TO LIVE. She looked around, and all she saw were people making up stories to create life… to justify being here, to justify taking another breath. What other choices did they have? She couldn't do it anymore. She simply could not do it anymore. She put down the pen, hating every word on the page. She was cut off from the world as surely as if she had no limbs - no arms or legs - only a core that could not move without assistance, and no one was there to pick her up, to move her through space. She had more in that core than universes combined, but she was a distant star with light years to the nearest planet, TO HERSELF. So she hung in her endless space of time and darkness until she felt her light diminish. Why use up her energy to shine when no one was there to see or feel her warmth. She felt the end coming.

Before this moment she knew everything could change in an instant, and she held on to life, but now there was only endless space, a void, a black hole, and she had been sucked into it. No techniques of empowerment worked because the Black Hole was more powerful, and she was alone. She was at the mercy of archetypes so powerful that she felt like a speck of dust blown by the slightest breeze. In death only would she be at peace. That was what she sought, not life in its endless struggle. And yet the sick joke was that if she chose to end it – she would only be plunged into it again, yet another lifetime to LEARN OR FIGURE OUT how to live.

She had tried to learn the lessons – to know the truth. She had a perception of what love tasted like, felt like, but she didn't know. She had a wealth of knowledge, but she didn't know. She had touched Jesus, Mary, the Goddess, the Devil, and countless other spirits, but she didn't know. AND SHE NEEDED TO KNOW! She was tired of living life unconsciously. That was hell, and she had enough of a taste of heaven to know that heaven was what she wanted. Did she have to get what she wanted?

～

---

2   Vol. III, p 158.

In a sudden flare of anger, I shouted, "Yes, I deserve to get what I want for no other reason than I have enough guts to want it. There are things worth dying for. Anything less is not enough. My will is strong; my heart is open; my spirit can soar, and I WANT WHAT I WANT."

All this time I had sat immobile, holding the knife, and struggling with its intent. I was wearing down. Something had to move. I visualized the knife plunging into my midsection over and over until my body jerked as if the knife had finally had its way. I let go and accepted the finality. "Where is my family?" I screamed.

I was immediately catapulted into a vision of myself lying on a stone floor in a pool of my own blood. I knew it was me, but I was dressed in something akin to burlap, the dress of a pauper or monk. Circled around me were human forms donned in white robes. They were moving to the left, shuffling their feet in some sort of dance or step. I remember EACH RIGHT FOOT was entering the circle crossing TO THE LEFT. Elongated faces with hair coming from the back of their heads. It was a ritual, not of joy but of somber dedication and reverence. They laid me on my back and began smearing blood all over my body. They took a white ash and powdered it on top of the blood. They painted a yellow circle on my forehead in the third eye region, and wrapped me in a garment of lavender with crystals sown into the fabric. I was carried to a stone table as other preparations were performed. All the while I was watching from above. I sensed I had to leave this part of me here for healing or ritual or preparation for death. These beings were my family, and they had come to my aid.

CHAPTER 2

Walking Dead

Wings, healing outside time and space: body, moving in ancient memory....

I returned to my position before the knife took over its destiny. I rose from my chair, put away the knife, and began carrying out the simple functions of living… no emotion… no questioning. I made arrangements for future activities although I had no sense of a future. I was in limbo. I did re-enact the events leading up to this limbo, but only as a feeling tone, not as an analytical deduction. What was it about – the sound of that door closing? I had no idea. I just knew I had never experienced anything like it in my life. It had the sound of finality, of something sneaking up or away from me. It was a shock to my entire system of rational thought. The word "gone" echoed, faded, then diminished into a tomb of silence. HE WAS GONE, a figment of my imagination, an illusion, a spirit that had no substance no matter how much I wished otherwise. How quietly and unobtrusive had he left as if it were the most natural thing to do, leaving me with the package he had dropped off at my door. Most natural – the package belonged to me – I must have signed for it, and he left to deliver other packages, no doubt. But for what had I signed? Had I opened the package, or did it still remain unopened in the doorway where I had lain before his exit. As he delivered words that made the relationship impossible, I left my body, and that body crumbled to the floor. I had seen the signs, but I needed to believe otherwise. I needed to give myself the chance to love again. I couldn't live with my skepticism and fear any longer; I needed to believe someone could truly love me. I was tired of broken promises and unfulfilled dreams. I was 55 years old, a woman, and a struggling artist. I was weary of rejection, WHETHER IT WAS FROM THE WORLD OR MYSELF.

She remembered reading the letters of Vincent van Gogh,[3] and she felt a kinship, especially now. She picked up the book, and felt his emotion about not being cut out for a "martyr's career." She felt his frustration about experiencing something which he had not intended. Somehow the words on the page and his presence cut through the numbness.

SHE RESONATED WITH HIS FRUSTRATION; SHE WAS TIRED OF THE "CROSS." A SPARK OF FIGHT WAS STILL IN HER.

"I need rest and relaxation – a vacation," she said. – trying to let the possibility penetrate. Concepts are obscure little creatures hiding under rocks from the light of discovery. Purpose is an illusion created for self-importance. Spirituality works only if you totally let go or transcend the fear. "I can't say I'm depressed, just indifferent and detached. 'Just is' doesn't quite fit or 'resigned' either. What is it? Silence."

Myriad of mysteries layered one on top of the other with billions of possible solutions or explanations. I walk through it, overwhelmed at the explosions of growth in one square inch. It's not a growth that has joy or order or fascination; it's a growth that is fraught with mutations and imbalance and frenzy. The growth is seeking to destroy itself – to start over in a responsible, directed, natural way. GROWTH FOR GROWTH'S SAKE IS NOT GROWTH BUT A STATEMENT IN SCARCITY. I never could stand the stillness when it appeared that nothing was growing – it felt like death - like there was no hope. Strangely enough I don't feel wounded or desperate or victimized. Maybe "this" is what they call "balance." Less pressure, less "have-to's", "should's" – more "What's the point." Maybe I'll be able to totally "feel" the moment – like what's going on – legs propped up cradling the paper on which I write. Fingernail polish chipped and multi-colored. Weight resting in the curve of the chair that has been my refuge, the chair destined to be there when I can no longer thrash my body through space and time, the chair quietly waiting to see when I fall, to see when I seek support, to see when I let go, the chair offering itself as structure but absorbing what I collect and bring back to it. So have I fully lived the moment writing? Do I know what its gift and price are? The pillow with its creases and shadows – just as important, I dare say, as the stock market with its dips and rises. There is silence waiting in every object, waiting for discovery, for observation so that it can perform its duty and go. The air is cool, flowing across my legs. My heels are hot from my morning walk. My left jaw hurts, and my neck is strained. I wonder, "What's the point?"

⌐⌐

She tuned in to Van Gogh's spirit and realized the futility of asking such a question. He had found it of relatively no significance to "insist" on an awareness of our "position" in life. He had

---

3   Vol. III, p. 163.

ceased asking certain questions that were a waste of time; the matter at hand was "living," no matter how obscure the meaning. From him came the courage to let go of the questions that lead nowhere.[4]

Message from The ~ Angels ~

You are entering the phase where such a question is irrelevant; you are in a minute microcosm of an immense universe. Your path will be made known as you walk to the other side of the question. (2013) [5]

My thoughts return to the cave that housed the white-robed figures... the ones who received me in my darkest hour. On the table where I had lain was now a beautiful woman, eyes closed, motionless. What had I done? Who was this woman -– was she alive or dead? The others watch over her, waiting, and I, too, knew I had to wait, to return at a later time.

I return to my waking consciousness. I busy myself with cleaning my environment – the house and car along with getting food and emptying trash.

I sit in my chair; and as I sit, I begin to have a desire to "know" this woman in the cave, whom I have named Kyalaka. I know she is there because of my actions. I feel responsible and connected to her in some inexplicable way. I journey to see her and find her just as I left her, lying on the same stone table. She wears a headdress, and there is a LUMINOUS GOLDEN LIGHT SURROUNDING HER HEAD. Even though I don't know "her story", I am filled with compassion and appreciation for her. I kneel beside her body. I am struck by her beautiful elongated face. I soothe her brow – touch her cheek and caress her chin. I pick up her hand – long, elegant fingers – lifeless now with no intent. I begin sobbing, holding her hand between both of mine. "What is your story, Kyalaka? How did you get to this place? Were you driven to take your life, or did you give it willingly for some higher purpose? I love you, Kyalaka. Please come back to me. Share yourself with me and I will share myself with you. I want to know you." In that instant, I feel a hand from behind me lightly touch my right shoulder. There stands a male in GOLDEN LIGHT. The figure looks like one of my guides, but has the essence of one of my sons. Not expecting anyone, I turn away, confused, and leave once again.

The door opens – I let the cat in – and she proceeds with her unchangeable ritual. I am envious, in a way, of a cat's habitual relationship with the door. Unlike her, my life changed drastically with the opening and closing of that door. I remember. My lover stands in front of the door, and before

---

4   Vol. III, p. 295.

5   In 2013, I began receiving messages about my book from Archangel Michael and other sources. I simply label these messages ~ Angels ~

he passes through it, he says, "There are three reasons why you shouldn't kill yourself." I sarcastically reply, "Why – because I'll just have to do it all over again." He says, "That's the third reason, the first two are your sons. They are your greatest masterpieces. Am I right?" I hear a gasp coming from my lips as if someone struck a blow with such force as to press all the air out of my body, and that body falls to the floor again. I have no sensation as to how I got from Plan A to Plan B.

I decide to check in on Kyalaka. I kneel beside her and beseech her to respond. I hear a voice reply. *"This is the Land of Dreams. I am Kyalaka, Guardian of the Crystals. I let my people down. They entrusted me with the crystals, but I failed. There was only one thing left to do – kill myself. With my death, the truth (a white feather falls from the wall in Mya's house) will be known… that no crystal is worth the essence of life. In dying – I will live again to protect that essence. My job is done for here and now. I have done what I can, and now the forces will play themselves out, enabling the drama to unfold. Jesus was not the only spirit who gave his life for humanity. I lived and breathed an earthly life to share my essence, to walk the path, to manifest. I have no regrets, and I am certain that my death is what is needed in this moment of time. I do not feel violence toward myself or judgment. My act is one of love, one of compassion. My brothers and sisters understand this. They prepare me, watch over me, and comfort me. I am not alone. Death by sacred knife is not an ordinary death, but one of sacrifice and compassion. Hear my words, Mya, you are not going to die yet because you carry the seed essence of life like I did. Your destiny is unfolding. Nothing can stop it now - no quirk of nature, no mistiming, no intervention. You can rest assured you will triumph in more ways than you can imagine. You will find the love you seek. Events will start to mirror what I am saying, and, know this, I will be by your side. You are not alone. I can feel you, see you, taste you. You are as dear to me as the Beloved. With wings outstretched, we will soar unfettered by earthly concerns. I am you, Mya. We are the same. Do not think of the future or worry about the mundane – you will be assisted. YOU HAD TO SEEK ME FOR THE NEXT STEP TO OCCUR. Know that you are firmly on the path.*

I retorted, "But what of the crystals – you say no crystal is worth the seed essence of life, and yet you took your life." Kyalaka smiles knowingly, *"I did not take my life, it was given by me. The crystals are but a reflection, Mya; they have no power of their own. They reflect the best and worst of all of us. To reflect the worst is as valuable as reflecting the best. Doing so helps us see clearly so we can live conscious lives. I did not take my life – I gave it."*

I was having trouble understanding and asked, "But why did you feel it was necessary? What purpose did it serve?" Patiently, Kyalaka continues, *"No other purpose than the willingness to give it. People prize life above all else. When they see someone willingly give that life, they are filled with gratitude and modesty. I ask, "Modesty? What does that have to do with it?" She says, "MODESTY IS THAT QUALITY THAT ALLOWS THE SOUL'S PURPOSE TO EMERGE. They are lifted above their ordinary lives."* "But what about the physical union of man and woman?" *I ask.* Kyalaka smiles, *"You will achieve it; trust me, it's part of your path. Do not be forlorn – you will be fulfilled. And you will inspire people with your courage and fortitude." "But what about you?"* I demand. *"I live in you, Mya. There is no difference. Don't you feel me?"*

Mya thought for a moment and replied, "Yes, in a way, I don't feel like the old Mya, but I am disoriented and lost." Kyalaka laughs, *"You are not lost; you are found. You just don't know what that entails. You have never been lost, even in your darkest hour."* "But I don't know who I am," I rebuked. Kyalaka took my hands in hers and said, *"You are Kyalaka, Van Gogh, Kandinsky, and many others."* I pulled back saying, "But don't I need a core personality?" She sat back allowing me some space and said, *"You have one – Mya. Mya is a spirit – you allowed her in to assist your child self, and she has done a good job. Your child is as powerful as you are now. Power is the ability to transcend. You have that ability – you've proven it time and time again. No other proof is necessary. Joy and peace are transitory; power is never-ending. You can have joy and peace if you let go of your old story. Live, Mya, and be happy in your accomplishment. You have succeeded beyond your wildest imagination."*

I was overwhelmed by all of this information, but I had to ask one more question. "Since I know you now, how will I be different?" She touches her heart and says, *"Your joy and abundance and innocence will be magnified."* Well, somehow I was complete with this last bit of knowledge, and Kyalaka and I embraced as we said our farewells.

It was almost as if Kyalaka connected me to Van Gogh, and I remember his feelings about how there was "no hope" for him unless he surrendered totally and eternally to this love for Kee that had entered his heart, and that this "real" love, in turn, created more "reality" in his drawings.[6] I felt the same way about the love I had for my two sons. My paintings were an extension of that love.

Message from The ~ Angels ~
Kyalaka is your "oversoul." She is your higher self, your unique divinity....your spark.
She holds the wisdom and the grace and the absolute beauty of your soul.

2013

During this period of time while Kyalaka was in limbo, Mya was more active than usual physically. She found no emotion to living, so she found it easy to take care of the business of routine tasks. She was operating on a robotic level with no sense of meaningful participation. She washed, polished,

---

6   Vol. I, p. 260, 261.

and waxed her car, even replaced parts – thinking briefly that she was scrubbing down to the surface of HERSELF, removing dirt, scum, and grime, and when that was impossible, acknowledging the residue as a scar or wound that couldn't or shouldn't be removed because it identified her. She put new windshield wipers on so that she could see as clearly as possible. She vacuumed the inside, finding food that had not decomposed, only hardened to a "petrified" state. She scrubbed, inspected, caressed. She experimented with products that worked and didn't work. She asked others for advice on how to care for the parts – how they worked and how they could be returned to their purest state. She used cloth, paper, and her hands to chip, peel, scrape, and rub off anything that didn't seem to belong there. She noticed that her tires were worn (growth that had taken its toll), and her paint job was marred from the tree sap (that which had fallen on her), and her grill had a concrete substance on it that couldn't be chipped off (that of which she couldn't let go).

Every once in a while she was aware of her body as she moved in different positions. She defiantly claimed her own body as off-limits to any man who intended to abuse her or take her for granted or render her invisible. She listened to angry songs about broken relationships and emotional bankruptcy and shallow involvements, cold renditions of what was once deemed a love affair. Hearts were not in danger because hearts had not been touched. "Just a misunderstanding," he said.

After the car, she began on her house, cleaning out the refrigerator which had rotted food and scum that was rock-hard. She scrubbed the cigarette film off the walls and cabinets and tackled the tub and sink. She threw away; she re-grouped, she filed; and she prioritized. She confronted, cajoled, and maneuvered. There was a part of herself that was unemotional, practical, and extremely efficient. There was no joy or satisfaction, fatigue, or completion. There was just movement.

She knew she was not "all home" because she began crying when she heard a phrase "taking you home" on the radio. She felt someone and something was taking her home, that strong hand reaching out to hold hers and to guide her. She was weak from the shock, the over-working, and the grieving. All she knew was that she loved the idea that someone cared if she went home or not, that someone understood. Desperately seeking angels, wisdom, and courage, she was now dead inside – stripped down to the surface (like the car) – not sure who she was, only feeling purified somehow, like the ashes after a fire. All she knew was that she was here – not happy or sad because of it.

CHAPTER 3

The Secret

Nothing would ever be the same again.

The door opens and closes. The cat meows. Mya was really getting tired of that damn cat meowing because every time it meant she would be entering another dimension where all the rules were different. Mya sits - the cat is out - and now she dreams of Van Gogh.

1890

The door closes. The ceremony ends. All the people have shuffled out of the small room that holds the casket of Vincent Van Gogh. I can feel Theo's heart breaking. He and Vincent were brothers but more that, they were twin souls of a sort, joined together by mysterious bonds. I feel Theo's reluctance to carry on without Vincent, his abject sorrow, his deep regret (that it had to end this way).

Everyone has said his or her good-byes to this "man of the soil." I question such an ending to a man who had given so much. What did he need he didn't get or have? What will it take for him to love again? Where is his soul wandering?

Kyalaka: *You haven't lost him. There will be a NEW DAY IN THE SUN!*

1982

The door opens. Mya decides to paint a painting honoring her favorite artist, Vincent Van Gogh. She is 37 years old and has been painting for 9 years. She never really considered herself an artist, but she did love it so. She felt she had no talent per se, just an ability to learn techniques and an ever-ending fascination with the process and the colors. She selects several of Van Gogh's works and plans a collage, intending to combine her style with Van Gogh's, not copying his work directly. As she begins painting, something happens she can't explain.

⚊

All of a sudden I begin breathing heavily. I have the sensation of running in the woods in fear of whatever is chasing me. There is panic and desperation to escape. "They" will eventually catch me and I will die. I pull away from the painting, looking away, trying to get a grip on what is happening. I decide to explore by beginning to paint Van Gogh's portrait. I copy the strokes, keeping the reproduction in front of my eyes. Suddenly a familiarity comes over me – I know these strokes – I know these colors. I know what comes next. All this time I am breathing as a panting animal running in the woods. I finish the portrait, and pick up the reproduction once again. THEY ARE ALMOST IDENTICAL! I go to sign Vincent's name, and again I know how to print the letters. I sit dazed in front of the canvas with a million questions pounding in my head. I was shocked, and yet elated. It was as if I had found someone I loved, someone I knew from the core of my being, someone who I thought was dead. I felt so honored to have stumbled upon this discovery, so joyous, so privileged. I was a child again believing that everything would be all right, that God was in his heavens, and I was in his palm. All my fears and doubts vanished in this ecstasy. I walked away and I carried the secret of what had happened in my Van Gogh experience, but it gave me strength - gave me a faith that things aren't as they seem. Nothing would ever be the same again. I talked to only a few about my experience, and they had rational thoughts to explain what happened, but I knew there was more to the story, much more.

The following years demanded more of me than exploring my experience and MY SECRET. Besides I had no one who could help me find the truth. I continued painting and rearing two sons and trying to make a distant relationship with my husband work. I filed my "moment" in the recycle bin of my mind.

Several years later I reluctantly moved to another house. As I put the paintings in the van, I couldn't seem to stop crying. The room in which I painted was my private world apart from everything else. That room was where I allowed myself to discover who I really am. The LOVE I knew for my children gave me hope and motivation and strength to continue the search. But now that search seemed uprooted, and my safe place was left behind. I moved again in three years, and the paintings and my soul found it difficult to find a resting-place. After all, having a place to paint was not a priority for some, but for me- my life's blood depended on it.

CHAPTER 4

The Mask

Who am I, this shell of a body walking, running, hiding?

2000

Mya prepares to teach mask-making to kids in a summer camp. By this time, she was as absorbed in Van Gogh's life as much as her own. In making her own mask, she reflects on the person behind the mask:

"Who am I, this shell of a body walking, running, hiding?" All the feelings and emotions of a thousand lifetimes - bringing my attention to moment after moment of experience. Who is this "I"? My greatest nightmare is when I shut out even the least of these "I's". My soul longs for wholeness and completion – to begin life – to wake out of the dream of separation. Why is it so difficult to wake from the dream? The nights are the most difficult because in the dark and in the dream reality, "I's" come forward demanding to be recognized on a stage of endless characters. As morning breaks, the curtain falls once more, and I am faced with no script, no costume, and no stage director. I look around at the limited space of my "script," and I am challenged to perform the extent of my experience. I drive down the street and see countless other people in their "plays". Which act are they in and which role has captivated them? I want an audience for "my play"; at the same time I want to practice my role in the dark until I can perfect my lines. When I DO execute my lines and receive blank stares from the audience, I retreat further into that darkness. The spotlight scares me, and yet I know I need the light.

There is no script, and the light will shine on my improvisation of the moment, but not before. Surrounded by rules and regulations of one small stage and the restrictions of one single character suffocate me, because I am much more. HOW CAN I EXPRESS THE TOTALITY OF LIFETIMES OF EXPERIENCE IN ONE COLOR OR ONE ROLE? And where is that damn director? What does he expect of me? Is he aware of the complexity and the breadth of my range?

Will he work with me to bring forth more of what I am, or reduce me to less than I am? What does my soul want? What does the audience want? I realize that I don't have a clue what the audience wants, and in trying to give them everything, I have given them nothing.

Then another realization seeps in, as if God were responding to my confusion. *"Until you find out what you want, I will give you all these experiences and opportunities to lead you to your "nemesis." Your job is to decide what you want. The instant you decide, your script will be written. And your success will depend on your acceptance of the role you have chosen. If you surrender to the character and become whom you are portraying, the audience will see you in the light and recognize the truth of your performance. When they leave the darkened theater and go out into the streets, they will know themselves better, and the light of that knowledge will shine into the darkness of their repressed desires and dreams. And the director will smile and realize he has become "more" than he envisioned, and his play will continue to create more Gods and Goddesses to perform their "magic" in the arenas of countless universes. Who do you want to BE – come?"*

CHAPTER 5

Kingdom of Heaven

Birds of a feather flock together.

Mya's ideas of the mask and the roles on stage took her back to the beginning of creation and the creator. She had been introduced to the idea of God and Heaven, and she now questioned the ideas floating around from different thought circles. She began to scan these theories to find what rang true for her. She writes:

~

Metaphysics tell us "like attracts like energy." The New Age tells us we are Gods; religion tells us "The Kingdom of Heaven" is within. (Luke 17:21). Some theories suggest that nothing exists without someone to observe it. On some level – Van Gogh does not exist for me until I observe his life and tell the truth of what I observe. I do not exist without Van Gogh's hope for the future, his dreams of an artist's community, his desire to share his work with other artists, and his need to find love. THE BOND IS UNBREAKABLE. Like energy attracts like. Van Gogh's life reveals issues of which I am concerned - the close relationship between music and art, the importance of emotions, the sorrow of rejection, the magic of color, the healing grace of the earth, the need to be of service to humankind, and the exhaustible proof that we are more than we can ever imagine. On this premise alone, Van Gogh and I had to meet outside space and time to exchange views. New Age points to our Godhood. What better proof that we are creators and Gods than to look at how we create our reality by every thought, word, and action, and if we are Gods and we are constantly changing and creating – then a "static" and "never changing" God does not exist. We are not powerless. We have within the ability to know what is best for us and we can be responsive to our innate knowledge about love and light. Van Gogh's rage and supposed insanity are not outside the realm of "Godhood" but actually crucial in the evolution of Gods. His rage is as holy as the music of the spheres. His rage comes from a tortured animal held in chains with no food. His rage transcends culture's rules and regulations and points to a greater truth. HIS RAGE REFLECTS HIS WISDOM ABOUT THE LOVE OF FREEDOM.

The Bible says, "The Kingdom of Heaven is within you." And yet those who would swear that the Bible is true renounce this fact everyday of their lives by setting up criteria, roadblocks, and obstacles undermining the grandeur of this revelation by prejudices, by selfishness, egotism, and elitism. Why would any philosophy or religion have to be taught, enforced, or spread if this statement were true? Why would there be "holy wars" or persecutions or enslavement of any kind if this statement were true? Why would any dogma or elaboration be necessary? Support for self-discovery would be the only criteria. Why would any label be necessary if this statement were true? Our cells have memory of the truth, but only through acceptance of all our parts (our darkness and light) can the body know itself and recognize the "Kingdom of Heaven". Anything less is HELL.

By observing Van Gogh, I began to realize that parts of myself WERE at war, and I longed for home, for peace. I didn't lack vision or a perception of love; I lacked acceptance of all my parts.

And what of Van Gogh, had he made progress in accepting his parts in spirit, discovered incantations or incarnated in other forms?

CHAPTER 6

Soul Retrieval

Shadows chasing shadows...

1998

I am sitting in my home in Oregon. Restless, I think of all my paintings in the loft… my life stacked in neat little rows above my head. The colors and shapes hovering as if in another time and dimension, waiting for eyes that could see. I had crated my "children" and moved them place to place, storing them for some unknown purpose. What were these "children" seeking – a home? A family? They were not full-grown yet and needed nurturing, love, shelter, and safety. SAFETY. Why did I feel I had to protect these creations and why did I feel threatened when I had to move them.

Suddenly I was thrust back in vision to my home in Oklahoma. The house was empty now. No remnants of my life remained. But there was an eerie stillness, a shadow of what had been. I had left something here – I knew – something that belonged to me. I frantically went from room to room searching. Then I entered the dining room that had been my studio, and I felt a presence there… a spirit… a guardian. This space, this safe place, this haven where I had painted had not let go of a part of me. Letting go would mean I had moved on, but I hadn't. I had remained here where I found Van Gogh, where I had compartmentalized my relationship with myself. How does one walk away from such a discovery, such a revelation?

How does one move all that energy to another place. I realized I hadn't and that I had to attempt to do so, even though 6 years had passed. I heard a rustle, and there before the easel I saw myself still painting. Embracing the shadow of myself, I gently pulled it into me and welcomed it home. "We have a new home now," I said. "Come with me. The work is safe." I looked around, and the room had lost its expectancy and restlessness. The room was still and peaceful, no longer caught between the past and future... just a room with no tearing emotions and grief. THE DOOR CLOSED.

Mya sat, stunned, looking at the pine trees outside her window. How had this happened? Why had she left part of herself in that house, in that room. And then emotion seized her, and she realized that the room was an entrance to another time and place, and she had believed she needed to stand guard there because she might not find an entrance somewhere else. She had discovered Van Gogh there – would she find him somewhere else? **Shadows of herself chasing shadows of herself.** Would she ever feel complete and safe and secure? She knew 6 years had passed before she had retrieved this part. How many more parts of herself came and went through time. Somewhere she felt that they all were performing functions in some space and time and returning when the situation demanded. She walked out of that house once more, this time in peace and without her heart being pulled asunder... 6 years of healing.

I AM The Angel of the East

I AM
The Angel of the East.
I see the sun rise and the sun set. My arms are welcoming to those who want to see the
light from the center of their divinity, from the Center of their Souls. I will be with you
through the dark times to show you the way to that which you have lost. I stand guard
over the earth making a bridge between earth and sky, shining through all eternity.

CHAPTER 7

What's in a Name?

If you call my name and see me, I will come. If you call my name and see another, I will go.

We have all experienced feeling projections and expectations placed upon us by friends and family. Sometimes, I wanted to scream: "Don't you see me - who I really am?" I am not my mother or my father or any relative or anyone on this earth. I am Mya - why can't you see me?"

I took on those projections and made them my own because only a thin veil existed between their reality and mine. I had always had this "thin skin." But when I lived in the reality of the thoughts of others and their images of me, I became lost and felt darkness surround me, my identity stolen.

I often thought of how a child comes into the world. Does that child have any expectations? Does it know if it will be loved or not? Does it know if it will be SEEN. What does it take for someone to reject culture, parents' beliefs, religion, and social structures to stand in their own right. How do they maintain their visibility?

Mya's thoughts turn to Van Gogh and the courage it must have taken him to keep walking on his path in the sun in the midst of so many storms, in the midst of so much rejection from those who expected something other than what he was, who wanted him to be who they wanted, not who he really was, who expected his message as a pastor and as a painter to be what was an acceptable interpretation of the customs and norms of his day. I wondered about his soul's journey - why he would choose such an incompatible time and purpose? What did he hope to learn, to experience, to REVEAL? And how did he hold onto his identity in the midst of such influence and pressure? Vincent's brother, Theo, wrote a letter to his mother and said what a remarkable book it would make to show the expansiveness of Vincent's thoughts and how through it all "he remained himself."[7]

---

7   Vol I, p. xii.

1992

I, Mya, lie on the table waiting for the massage therapist to enter the room, wondering what secrets my body would reveal. The door opens. Rasha begins working on my back and shoulders. All of a sudden out of nowhere, I say, "My mother never loved ME." The words sound strange coming out of my mouth; a finality resides there (as if this truth has existed over all time). I cry bitter tears as the emotion sweeps over my body. My back is hurting, but somehow I know the wound is in my heart, and that wound is ageless. Rasha provides some relief to the pain, and my tears provide some cleansing.

Afterwards, I reflected about my Mother, and I realized that she loved me in the way she only could love me - to love me from her perspective of who I was, as a daughter, as a part of a German family (complete with all its traditions, scope, and preferences). She loved me from all that she knew or had experienced, but I sought more. I was not part of a group; I was not a "name." I was not a reflection of some conceptual collection of truths and half-truths. I was "me," and I thought and felt outside all those ideas and beliefs, and I wanted to be seen for my heart-felt thoughts and aspirations.

THE DISCREPANCY BETWEEN WHAT WAS AND WHAT I DESIRED WAS STORED IN MY MUSCLES, MY RANGE OF MOVEMENT, IN MY ABILITY TO EXIST WITHOUT PAIN.

My mother had named me Michelle Angelo after the famous artist Michelangelo. From the very beginning I lived in the shadow of someone else – someone who had a reputation – someone who had gained acceptance. I was teased and prodded about my name. Attention was always drawn away from me to some "other". I was never just Michelle; so when I left home, I revised and shortened my name to "Mya."

CHAPTER 8

The Soul of an Artist <u>(Breaking the Rules)</u>

**Going into the pain releases you from the bondage of your
attachment to the story you have created around it.**
~ Angels ~

August 2000

<u>From the journal of Mya:</u>

My whole life I have been afraid of breaking the rules. I have been afraid that I would break a rule either because I didn't know the rule or because I could not do otherwise. There were so many rules: social ones, religious ones, moral ones – on and on. I held some illusionary belief that if I followed all the rules, I would be safe. Nothing was farther from the truth.

We are taught to control our emotions. Don't get too angry - too passionate - DANGER DANGER DANGER. And yet our emotions are what make us human, what enable us to have compassion. Our emotions instruct us when we are betraying ourselves, when our hearts are breaking, and when we are grieving. Suppressing these emotions creates deadness, and the deadness creates more deadness. I have seen so many people who do not allow themselves to feel for fear of losing control or the pain it may bring. My "thin skin" has always somehow allowed me to feel another's pain, and so many of my tears have been shed simply because another could not.

I felt deeply - just as Van Gogh wanted to be known for that same quality - and I sought to express that in paint, a language that was not limited by the conscious mind. I was seeking a vessel that would contain the emotions and still be capable of balance and serenity. I looked at Van Gogh's paintings and wondered if our goals were the same. We both were "obsessed" with opposites. Mine were male/female, left/right brain, colors, etc., and the balance of the painting that pointed toward wholeness… wholeness that was born out of love.

Reading the Van Gogh letters, I noticed so many entries about love and nature, and I felt the passion of his love. A chill runs up my spine, and his presence comforts me, confirming our kindred spirits and telling me of his love, his compassionate "eye" for all things.[8]

So maybe to love in such a way was all ABOUT breaking the rules. I didn't want what I could control; I wanted what needed to materialize, and I had no words for it. At first I was simply confronting the opposite of love: fear. I was reveling in the victories, but then something else took over, a knowing, an unconscious wellspring flowing from my brush that transcended all thought. I became addicted to what I didn't know, what was in the wellspring. When the mysteries were revealed, I felt elated and so thrilled and satisfied. At that point whatever it took to get to that moment was worth it and then some. However, when I struggled or tried to think my way through, I couldn't get there, couldn't find the way to the magic and mystery.

When my mind couldn't get out of the way, and I exhausted myself trying to CONNECT, I became despondent, and my whole world for days on end was shrouded in darkness. I felt so forlorn, so destitute, feelings of losing EVERYTHING. I had everything, and now it was all gone. My beloved was gone, and I walked through my world like a ghost with such emptiness and longing. It was a grieving - of existing in the highest love and light and then in one split second becoming conscious of all of it being gone.

I walked through the park, thinking of all the artists that had ever lived, and I felt that I carried their imprint... THEIR IMPRINT LIVED INSIDE OF ME - THEIR SOUL'S PURPOSE. So much was at stake here. I could not explain the depth of this emotion to myself or anyone else, although I tried on a few occasions. I felt totally alone. Thank goodness, these periods were usually short, and I came out of it. I sometimes wondered if the feelings resulted from my own judgment of myself for not being able to touch the power that I knew was there. Or could it be a purging - a going through the darkness or murkiness to get to the light, enabling the experience of light to be magnified and wholly transcendent. I reminded myself of what I read in 'Shamans, Healers, and medicine Men "by Holger Kalweit -.... "shamanism is closely connected with suffering. One must suffer the disintegration of one's own system of thought in order to perceive a new world in the higher space." p. 4

I continued to go thru these painful, dark times when I painted...resting in between, recovering. The brush in my hand seemed to be the key to opening the door to this upheaval... this entering an alternate universe with different realities, different structures, different languages.

I entered this world when I felt strong enough or mustered up the courage. Not all journeys were fraught with difficulty or pain, but often I had to pass through an "initiation" before I released the power within and relieved the "angst."

---

8   Vol. I, p. 416.

From "Crystal Woman" by Lynn Andrews. Ginevee says, "You have learned to study your own suffering so that the suffering of others could be understood. Teach your apprentices not to distract themselves from their pain. Lead them in the center of pain, to confront it."

Even though I felt the heart of past artists and their lives and was so appreciative of them all, I also felt that I would expand the heart cavity TO DREAM GREATER DREAMS.

Could such a link between artists over time be possible? Jane Roberts as Seth states that "the great artists have always been able to communicate." She states that time is not restrictive or experienced in the usual sense; therefore, the past speaks to the present and future, present to past and future, and future to past and present. She states, "Therefore, actions that you make now can help a so-call past personality; and a so-called future personality may step in and help you along your weary way."[9]

Van Gogh constantly spoke of past and future artists and kept them in his "range of vision" as he created in his day.

1998

I had been invited to join a group of artists who were striving to eliminate the blocks sabotaging their creativity and their ability to become the type of artists they desired. We used specific techniques and psychological inquiries to reveal what STORIES we had been telling ourselves about "who" we were and "what" had happened to us and "how" it had influenced our progress.

We were shown the energy invested in these stories and how our language imprisons us and keeps us in the "victim" stance. Changing these stories of powerlessness changes how our artistic expression unfolds!

When I was asked to <u>invent</u> a story that described my life and work, I surprised myself when I said, "Why, I am Van Gogh, of course, and I have come back to paint."

I didn't think much at the time of what I had said, but I felt empowered saying it. Could there be a passion so strong that it didn't die with one person or one time or one dimension? Could that passion manifest itself in a myriad of psychological and spiritual ways in hearts and minds that were open, rooted in individual personalities but transpersonal and universal at the same time?

I remembered Theo, Vincent's brother, talking about how Vincent's paintings would one day be "sublime." Did he see into the future to see the response by others to his paintings, or was there an underlying "knowing" that the energy of the paintings would morph into other forms and be raised to a higher vibration?

---

9   The Eternal Validity of the Soul, p. 279, p. 409.

Chapter 9

Dreams As Seeds

My dream, snuggly resting in the cosmic sac, waits for its time.

I began thinking of dreams and how they are born and die, and how the seeded dreams manifest in reality. I write:

Sometimes dreams are born but, just as plants, do not receive the water and sun needed for growth; dreams do not receive the flow of recognition and the light of understanding. Too much water or too much sun kills the dream.

The dream relies on eyes that see, ears that hear, and a heart that can be touched.

Dreams are like a natural childbirth. They can be born breech or cesarean. Whatever the method, pain is usually the common denominator. A successful birth renders exaltation. An unsuccessful birth renders sorrow and death.

Dreams are born in the time between the door closing and the door opening, a timeless space where anything is possible, the "crack in the universe."

The impetus to open this portal is usually motivated by great joy or great sorrow or extreme pain.

My thoughts motivated me to write this poem:

Mya's Dreamscape
Are there dreams worth dying for?
Are there dreams worth living for?
Are there seeds that must be planted?
Are there weeds that must be plucked?
Are there hearts worth saving?
Are there bodies worth purging?
Are there souls worth hearing?

Are there spirits worth soaring?
Is there a freedom that lifts all density?
That dispels all darkness?
That sings the highest note?
That creates new worlds?
To be free is to know bondage
And yet to shed the shackles
To be free is to be in captivity
And yet fly through the cage
To be free is to choose freedom
When the world wants to enslave
To be free is our inheritance
Waiting for our acceptance from Gods on High
To be free means the "all" returning to the "one"
To be free requires an open heart
The choice is YOURS!

Mya wondered what Kyalaka would say about dreams. She had almost forgotten her encounter with the sacred knife and the essence Kyalaka. So she asked: "What are dreams?"

Kyalaka: *Dreams are about your unlimited potential. This potential awakens in you the need to create scenarios in which these "gems" may be realized. Your heart knows: your mind forgets. Dreams are the heart's desire.*

Mya: What if the heart desires something out of balance or corrupt?

Kyalaka: *Smiling – You know the truth about this. Why do you paint?*

Mya: I paint to touch something I can't touch any other way.

Kyalaka: *And what is that?*

Mya: All that I am.

Kyalaka: *Which is?*

Mya: The shadow.

Kyalaka: *And what is the shadow?*

Mya: That which I don't know about myself. But what does that have to do with dreams?

Kyalaka: *Your dreams are a willingness to know yourself completely.*

Mya: But what if that is evil?

Kyalaka: *Love is the answer.*

Mya: What if people dream a dream <u>for</u> you?

Kyalaka: *It's not your dream.*

Mya: Can I dream a dream for all of humanity?

Kyalaka: *You set the stage for possibilities.*

Mya: But how do I know if that's appropriate? Why do I fall in doubt when I'm around other people.

Kyalaka: *Because they have another dream.*

Mya: But how can the two dreams co-exist?

Kyalaka: *Love – free will.*

Mya: But is there a "right" or "high" dream?

Kyalaka: *The only high dream is to be one with spirit. You can't control other's dreams – you can yours.*

Mya: What is the connection with Van Gogh?

Kyalaka: *To be able to have the freedom to dream your own dreams and not be forced to live another's.*

Mya: So are you saying I am living Van Gogh's dream?

Kyalaka: *No, I'm saying you are attracted to Van Gogh because IN ESSENCE HE IS "YOU." Your dream is not his, BUT EACH OF YOU RECOGNIZE THE OTHER'S HEART.*

Mya: But if we're all "one", why isn't there just one dream?

Kyalaka: *Because many have chosen to not see or to not wake from the illusion.*

Mya: Why would they choose such darkness?

Kyalaka: *To punish themselves because of their guilt.*

Mya: How does art fit in all of this? How can I sell my art if others don't share my dream?

Kyalaka: *Many do. Many have awakened. Mya, love shines in your paintings – you know that. You have the courage to see and to transcend the mass consciousness. The paintings lift – enlighten.*

Mya: What is the highest purpose for my creations? Where do I take them? Why can't I sell them?

Kyalaka: *You have to let go. You dream – you make it visible – and then you let go to dream another dream.*

Mya: But I always have to go back and try to sell the past dream.

Kyalaka: *Your dreams are futuristic – so the past dreams are the present.*

Mya: Thank you.

Kyalaka: *Dreams are seeds. Some seeds are buried so deep in consciousness that they are not even visible. Some seeds have worked their way up through time to be cracked open by space. Some seeds are held for thousands of years in the minds of genius, sometimes creating madness. Some seeds are lying on the earth's surface, waiting to be picked up by some winged creature to be taken to exotic lands. Some seeds are ingested by wolves and lose their shape and form, morphic and hidden from the light of day. Some seeds burst as soon as they recognize themselves as seeds. Some seeds are alchemically transformed through the heat of purification. Some seeds receive too much water or stare at a <u>hot sun of consensus, succumbing to the burning ash of</u>*

mediocrity. Some seeds are bombarded by fears of survival until they die an instantaneous death, suffer a long drawn-out death, or are carried out to sea.

Mya: Where do these seeds originate before they are thrown into destiny's soup? What is the seed essence of life? Where are these seeds born? Why cannot these seeds be promised one destination? Why do they seem to be blown by wind with no direction of their own?

Kyalaka: The seeds are light. LIGHT IS THAT PART OF EVERY SOUL THAT REMEMBERS.....LOVE.

Mya was tired of this conversation with herself, with every question leading to another one. She needed help understanding about love, light, and dreams. In her frustration, she demanded, "I'm tired of lesser Gods. I want to know who is in charge. I want to know if I agree with this power. Before I continue to be of service, I want to know what the plan is. Do I not sell my soul if I continue in service without knowing the intent of the one I serve? I am enraged that I have been kept in the dark."

Kyalaka: *You haven't, Mya. You have always been in the light. You have chosen darkness.*
Mya: Then how do I choose the light if I don't understand what I'm choosing?
Kyalaka: *You're choosing life, love, peace, and immortality.*
Mya: How can I be sure?
Kyalaka: *What do you feel?*
Mya: I do feel the light.
Kyalaka: *Aho! You have been afraid the light would be too bright. Like with Van Gogh.*
Mya: YES! How do I temper the light to what I can stand?
Kalaka: *It begins with love. If love is there, you will be protected. If not, you may be burned.*
Mya: So many words about love – what is it? I'm going in circles.
Kyalaka: *LOVE COMES IN WHEN YOU SURRENDER, WHEN YOU QUIT FIGHTING YOURSELF. Look at yourself, Mya. What do you see? Draw that image.*

Mya was pulled into a dream. *Van Gogh was dreaming, too. He was dreaming of having all that he needed, to paint, to have food and shelter, to be a part of someone's life, to be needed and have a sense of home - to realize his dream....dare he hope that such a thing existed...this type of freedom? She walked by his side, and whispered in his ear, "YES!" And the angels there told me that Vincent was a visionary - able to plant seeds, the bounty to be harvested in the future. He was the "sower."*

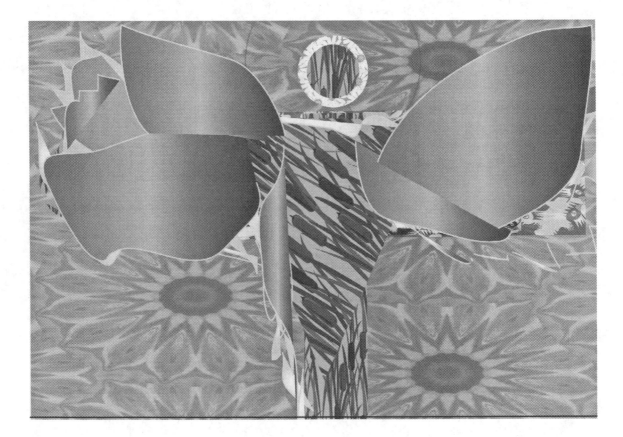

I AM

The Angel of Expansion.

I am about sunflowers, the golden mean - when it's time to grow and when it's time to rest. Always, I am reaching for the sun - for that which will provide the energy and strength to fulfill my destiny. The sunflowers teach me how to produce the seeds and dreams for future harvest.

CHAPTER 10

Painting the Sketch

**Color is the pathway to who we have been in the past and who
we are now and all the detours along the way.**

I unbury sketchbooks, frantically searching for a theme for my new show. Oh my – look at this one. How could I possibly have been able to portray that essence back then? And look at this one. This one is part of who I was becoming. What mystery and intrigue! I am always reluctant to remove these sketches from the compact, orderly sequencing - from the companionship of the other drawings supporting and encircling and clarifying my frame of mind, all in their own pockets of time. I feel my life being torn apart again. I feel myself being pulled out of control. I know change is in the air, and I tense as I wait to see what this new ordering has to say or reveal. What story will it tell?

This re-ordering - how like a soul that is transferred when the personality dies and is reborn in another timespan. The new personality has been changed, but there are traces of the old. The sketch has been buried in the earth where the flesh has dropped away, revealing the bones. The colors have faded and new ones added due to the earth's deposits. Rips and tears reflect the earth's own labor pains and funeral pyres. Another work of art has been born from the faint lines mapped out in the past. The new sketch or persona is both less and more than before. TIME HAS MADE ITS MARK.

I envisioned Van Gogh burying his sketch in the sands of time, and me going to the grave, unburying the sketch, imagining what it had been and what it needed to be now. I know that dreams do not die; people do not die; art does not die. All is a living, breathing transformation slipping through that passageway of all possibilities. I know that dreams will appear as sequential time frames clipped as from a movie. I'm not sure of the beginning or the end. All I know is that I have agreed to be a player in this movie and that for the first time I am really living on stage and not behind the scenes. I AM THE SKETCH BECOMING THE PAINTING!

August 1998

Mya now had her art degree and was contemplating undergraduate studies. She had created her paintings the last three years with academia breathing down her neck. She now wanted her art to be more self-directed and authentic. Many times as she painted, sections of the canvas would suddenly reveal "Van Gogh impressions", but usually she painted over them. Now she was tired of fighting what was there. So she decided to go there. She would surrender to the impulses and enlist the help of her "ancestry" - that's the word that formed in her consciousness, "ancestry." One such day, she set up her easel to paint, and…

The colors came furiously, but with decisive strokes and movement. "He" was here, and "I" was here in this strange moment out of time. I had been frightened before when I considered this, but now I was even more frightened of the power and surety. I was excited, yet intimidated; allowing Van Gogh to come through while astounded how natural and familiar the inclinations were. My mind had no place to put what happened when my brush hit the canvas. Confused, disoriented, but ecstatic, I put away my easel and painting supplies, searching for some rational explanation, some reason why the Van Gogh strokes placed themselves so effortlessly on my canvas and the color combinations were so in synch with my nature. I filed away the questions for another time.

Soon after this experience, Mya felt drawn to take a trip to the Southwest. Based on what had happened, she didn't know if she was running away FROM something or running TO something. However, she was certain that she needed the "light" in New Mexico. Maybe, she speculated, the light was close to the South of France where Van Gogh painted, or maybe THIS light was the next step in the discovery of a new ingredient in the light.

Even before she chose New Mexico as her home, she felt that Van Gogh was rooted there. She periodically sensed he had something to tell her or wanted her to do something, and he seemed adamant that she should, "PAINT!" When she could stand the intensity, she studied his life looking for clues.

Then Mya heard about a Van Gogh exhibit in L. A. and just HAD to go. Here is her account of the incident:

I am obsessed about getting to the exhibition even though I am terrified about traveling into LA, especially alone. After several failed attempts of getting a companion, I gear myself up to making the trip alone. Speaking of gears, my car at the last moment develops mechanical problems. I borrow a car with a stick shift of which I am totally unfamiliar and proceed into LA. I simply HAD to see that exhibition.

I arrive after a harrowing experience of shifting gears and managing traffic and signs. I am terrified of rolling back into another car because I couldn't manage the clutch and brakes in a timely fashion. I see the banners for the exhibition, and my heart skips a beat, several in fact. I project into what Van Gogh would think of this public display after his frustration to "be of some use." I enter the show, put on the earphones for the audio guide and enter the first room. The room is crowded (being the first day) and bodies are slowly shuffling around --all in their internal reflection, responding to what their eyes were seeing. There is a reverence here – a respect – and a need to understand. I suddenly am so grateful to these souls who came to pay their respect.

As I view the paintings, I am struck by the expertise, the sensitive and precise handling of the paint, and above all by the light emanating from each work. I round the bend, and there before me is one of the paintings of "the old shoes." I lose my footing for a moment as if I had tripped over the loose shoestrings. In a flash I remember my own painting of some old shoes, and suddenly the two paintings were transposed over each other, somehow comparably akin, somehow belonging one to the other. I continue on, but I kept feeling drawn back to the shoes. By now every space in the room is filled with a voyeur. Making my way back, I am stopped by a museum curator. "You can't go back – the exhibition is too crowded." Anger rises as I question whether anyone has the right to hold me back. I paid to see this exhibition, and was prepared to BREAK ANY RULE to see what I needed to see. I waive my impulse to crash or sneak through, but I remain doggedly loyal to my resolve.

Mya's painting of old shoes

I enter the last room, and by this time people are visibly moved. One woman, upon viewing one painting, turns away saying, "I can't look at it; there is absolutely no hope." Ten or fifteen people are half-circled in front of the "Wheat Fields With Crows." Some are outwardly crying; others are almost frozen by the effort to contain strong emotion. Over all, I sense some tribute, some honor, some recognition paid to this Van Gogh life of struggle. Perhaps humanity has become wiser to the nuances displayed by Van Gogh's hand. Perhaps their hearts are more open to the colors of his soul. Perhaps they needed, today, to embrace the love of a man humbled by grace.

I begin wiping the tears away, trying to control the strong emotion welling up inside of me. I observe as if I were two people, Mya and Vincent. Vincent is surprised by the response of the crowd, and Mya is the sentinel – the guardian for this rare happening. I question whether I want to go back into the other rooms, but decide I had received what was intended for me, but somehow I can't seem to leave the room, so I lean against the wall by the painting of the wheat fields. A curator promptly tells me I can't do so, but I accept that directive because in touching that wall, I fulfilled a purpose; that of "standing in" for Van Gogh and that of honoring the space. I take one more look and then leave the room, smelling the scent of sunflowers in bloom and feeling the sense of a completed destiny.

CHAPTER 11

A Life of Service

I would rather have you see me now than remember me later.

8-2000

Mya reflects on her experience as an artist, and she relives the bitterness she feels for the difficulty in acquiring a showplace for her work, dealing with the "art business" and the education of the public. She writes:

> "AN ARTIST IS CAUGHT BETWEEN TWO WORLDS: HIS
> VISION AND THE ACCEPTANCE OF HIS VISION."

By the law of integrity, some artists are bound to paint what they see or feel, and yet they are dependent on the scope of their viewers to earn a living. They sacrifice themselves to travel the extremes of emotion and open themselves to revelation, but their revelation is often deemed manic or judged by the norms of the day.

They open themselves to empathize with the lowest creatures, and they are often labeled depressive. They become one with passion, and they are often judged fanatical. They dress to suit their work, and they are perceived to be slovenly and unmannered. They give humanity all of themselves and more, and humanity responds often by making criticisms and diverting their eyes from the very honesty that could enlighten them. Sometimes these artists shrink from becoming well known, and the public might see their tendency as a sign of weakness or a "fear of success."

How easy for us to judge someone who is risking all to bring forth their truth. How easy for us to intellectualize and create fantasies and to veil that truth. How easy for critics, the public, the collectors to invent their stories and receive accolades for their clever presentations. And how easy to comment on the creations rather than to actually take up the sword or brush and take on the challenges and demands of the life of an artist. Walking inside the channels of creativity – dealing with the archetypes - opening and allowing the tearing down - re-building, inventing – opening to that which is beyond self is the way of the artist, and the words and commentaries at the artist's expense are cruel and unwarranted.

True creativity, like God, does not fit in a box. The great works of art are not to be mulled over and changed to fit a warped and unenlightened audience. Great works of art are from the beyond and come many times at great expense to the artists who bring them. And yet you (critics) play your games of superiority, of money, of manipulation, and dare to diminish the greatness of the work by your invented psychoses and cheapening strategies.

And, I asked myself, what if my art should become popular or sell, what "story" would be attached to the images. I feel protective of what I create. I don't want an elaborate string of pompous and pretentious verbiage by people pretending to know what is inside my heart, intent and psyche - to claim ownership of interpretation based on opinions which are only that - opinions… sterile and un-visceral, psychoanalyzing what drove me to make a stroke, to choose a color. How absurd!!!! I am not afraid of success; I am afraid that the success would be based on some "false hype" or attention to ONE detail, LIKE THE CUTTING OFF OF AN EAR when the soul and spirit of what I really had done would never see the light of day.

Some artists may want recognition of self in their endeavors, but others want true appreciation of the work itself. I wondered if it would give Van Gogh pleasure to know that his paintings (not sold in his lifetime) were worth billions of dollars now? I would think he would be pleased to some extent, but perhaps his greatest interest would be to have the money for MORE PAINT to continue to express his visions. IT WAS THE WORK THAT MATTERED, and no amount of words could adequately describe that passionate "knowing."

What is at stake here is not one soul but all the human souls that come from the "one." Art is the guardian of that which is soul. If we lose the expression and sharing of soul, we lose our HUMANITY.

⌒

Mya remembers her experiences through out the years of show after show, observing what seems to get the attention of the "status quo." She goes on another tirade, tasting the bitterness of the injustice she perceives:

"You say (mass consciousness) you support the arts by going to sidewalk sales, which have for the most part turned into circuses. You say you support the arts by buying paintings from artists who have agreed not to grow to support your lack of growth. You say you support the arts yet elect officials who censure the arts. But what do you do to keep inspiration alive? What do you do to support artists who have given their lives to support freedom? What do you do to see that artists who have given their lives for this cause have the minimum means of food, clothing, and shelter. There are more programs to protect wildlife and domestic animals from abuse and extinction that any to protect artists from same.

TRUE ARTISTS ARE AN ENDANGERED SPECIES.

True artists are the life and blood of revealing who we are in the midst of the robotic age that is upon us, the true imprint of our authenticity, the fingerprint, if you will, of what it means to be human.

Frank Herbert wrote Dune in 1965, a science fiction novel. Following were many other books in the series. In one of these books called Chapterhouse, set 21,000 years in the future, a spaceship leaves, and on board are people escaping domination and control, taking the bare essentials - the things that matter to start a new life elsewhere.

On board that spaceship is a treasured painting by Van Gogh called "Cottages of Corbeville.."... "only rare remnants such as this painting remained to send a physical impression down the ages."...

Others on board question why it is so treasured and coveted, and Odrade replies, "You asked for my hold on humanity and here it is."... "Look at it! An encapsulated human moment."... (page 85) And, I might add, in each stroke were the feelings of a human poised in real time, more real than reality itself.

You do not need a critic to tell you if a great work of art is before your very eyes. YOU HAVE ONLY TO SEE IT WITH YOUR HEART. A great work of art transcends the visual; it reaches out and helps you remember the truth. All you have to do is be willing to accept that truth – your truth. And when you do, show that appreciation in the value system presently in use, <u>money</u>."

I stare at the pages in my journal where I had ranted and raved at the injustice and hypocrisy. I surface enough to look at my own life. Battling anger for more years than I want to admit, I struggled to survive as a painter and still keep that "humanity" and "love" in my heart… to keep on doing the work I had been called to do without monetary support, without a patron or philanthropist.

In the past perhaps I wasn't visible enough, or dedicated enough, but over the years I corrected that. I followed all of the rules I could, and still I felt the dispassion and apathy of the audience at large. When I presented myself and my work to someone, I usually had to listen to their stories of other artists and how much money these artists were offered for a painting… almost as if someone exalted themselves by knowing in the world's terms a successful artist, while right in front of them is me - an "up close and personal" artist with raw experiences and stories that could give them an intimate look at an artist's life other than how much money they received for a painting, as if that amount of money was what they were worth as an artist. In the meantime, there I stood, smiling, validating their stories, while all the while I felt totally "invisible."

I had painted for 30 years and paid my dues. I believed in my work, and had many "experts" verify the high quality therein; and yet I was still forced to jump through hoops. Gallery owners dismissed me without hesitation, mumbling something about, "It's not what we're looking for." Or, "your work looks like sketches - come back in a year and let us see what you have done." Or, "let me show you this new technique or process" (with THAT PROCESS exalted instead of the quality of the actual work).

And of course, the other detraction is the adoration and morphed stories of artists who are dead. It's easy enough to support artists long dead, while living artists are starving for a chance. I know Van Gogh also felt that the "living artists" were ignored, (while) giving money to dead artists.

I held on to my self-respect and optimism, my belief that some day a door would open, but I cried behind closed doors, trying to keep my dream still vivid in my mind. I had learned to take care of myself through diet and exercise and meditation, but no one seemed to notice. It wasn't dramatic enough. I FELT I HAD ALREADY GIVEN MY LIFE ONCE, AND NOW BY CLAIMING MY LIFE, I FACED ANONYMITY.

Suddenly I realized that if I walked out into the street and sliced off my ear, people would notice and create a tragic story about my life, and perhaps subsequently my paintings would be in demand. I could join the circus of hype and trumped-up stories. Critics and collectors would sell the stories, and my work would be priceless. Or perhaps I could go to prison on some minor charge, and paint from prison – having some person, who needed a cause, come gather the paintings and sell them at large… of course resplendent with the TRAGIC STORY. Or if I was handicapped in some way and still managed to paint – surely that story would sell.

When will art be seen and sold for its inherent quality without the tragic story, without needing the artist to be crippled or insane or PR privileged. I suppose that "wholesome" is somehow boring to an insatiable audience, feeding on drama and gossip. WHAT IS THE VALUE OF A LIFE OF SERVICE? The door closes.

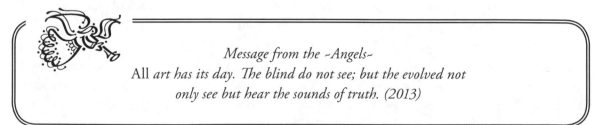

Message from the -Angels-
All *art has its day. The blind do not see; but the evolved not only see but hear the sounds of truth. (2013)*

My thoughts go back to dreams. In order for the dream to exist on earth, the dream must have a destination from the dreamer. As an artist, I enter the reality of my creation where ego is disintegrated. I literally become my creation. In order to root this creation, I have to return to some semblance of an identity. To say this is difficult is an understatement because I have seen with other eyes and felt with other hearts. I HAD BECOME LOST IN THE WHOLE.

As with a near-death experience, I didn't want to return to the density, to the lies, to the fear, to the greed. I am free- floating in an eternity of light and color. I am angry that I have to return to imprisonment. My spirit is soaring and now my wings are cracking and breaking. And yet I know I have to show others the dream. I have to let them know what is possible – what is "out there" or more accurately "in here." THE DOOR CLOSES - THE DOOR OPENS.

Every work of art, for me, is a death process that is freeing and uplifting followed by a birth process that is about loss and separation. Every time I step up to the plate (easel), I have to gather my courage to begin the journey. Then when I return with my representation, the painting of the journey, I ask myself – "What now? How do I sell the dream? Who wants to buy the dream? Who can even see the dream? What hearts are open to remember they came from "the dream?"

Eyes stare blankly as they view my work questioning whether I know or have any ability to paint or create form. They stare, as if threatened, only a short while, turning away quickly to attend to more important matters, such as 'where am I going to eat lunch?' They know how to feed their bodies, but not their souls. I try to remain unattached – I do not own the dream – I am only its caretaker. I myself do not have any articulation about the dream that makes any sense in the language of earth. I have trouble detaching FROM the work, but I know I can't live there yet. I HAVE TO REMAIN SEPARATE IN ORDER TO HOLD IT. I question what the purpose, meaning, or benefit is to such a dream when I know I can't exist in it yet. What benefit is it to anyone else?

And yet I know I am in service of some higher purpose, and I follow like a blind man walking through a world I can't see – only feel in my heart and soul. And I lament what price I've paid to keep the dream alive, and yet I've guiltily admitted that perhaps I would die for such a dream, and that death would be a small price to pay. Self doubt enters and makes me question whether the dream is an illusion and what I feel in my body the only reality. I feel like a fool who is seeped in idealistic notions and false inventions, and I feel like a failure who failed "reality 101."

But then I glance at a segment of a painting, and I recognize and remember another time, and I soar with hope and peaceful realities and complete assurance that I have touched something "real." And I continue doing the work, feeling privileged and cursed at the same time. I isolate and dream the dream. I am rich in experience and revelation. I am in the monastery of art and ideas, and I live a meager existence. I am as the Bible says "in the world but not of it," and I continually pray that my life and work is for the highest good of all. I AM HERE TO SERVE, AND MY HUMILITY DEMANDS THAT I ACCEPT WHATEVER PRICE I HAVE TO PAY. My small life is but a spark in the grand explosion of light from whence I came. I do not or cannot understand, but I follow.

CHAPTER 12

The Story vs. The Art

The paint tells its own story.

November 2000

Mya writes in her journal:

One thing I know is that art heals. "Art therapy" exists in our culture, but oftentimes it is rigid and categorical in its diagnosis. Often the wound is seen in the images, disregarding the "angels" present there.

Some wounds aren't visible. Some wounds are deep in the psyche and soul. Soul loss can be prevalent. Survival by fragmentation of self is common. I've told my story in my paintings to anyone who can see. The media, however, demands certain kinds of stories, the sensational and the absurd. If I grew two heads and painted, then I would really be something, but the truth is I do have two heads (and more) – many lifetimes. However, if you photographed me, you would see only one head, and people tend to believe only what they see. Yes, they can see if a person is blind – there is evidence – he or she has dark glasses – has a seeing-eye dog – walks with a cane. And paints- what a marvel! And they can see before them a picture of an elephant swinging his trunk picking up and choosing colors to create a composition. What a marvel -—and truly so, but what exactly is the purchase? Are they purchasing a work of art based on quality and transcendence or are they purchasing the story of an elephant painting?

I have a story, too, that demands you rethink what is possible, but I AM NOT CAGED. I DON'T HAVE A ZOO KEEPER OR FOOD BROUGHT TO ME DAILY. I DO NOT ROCK DRAGGING MY CHAINS. I ACTUALLY HAVE TO LIVE BY THE SALE OF MY PAINTINGS, BUT NO ONE SEEMS TO CARE ABOUT THAT! Is fear lurking in the viewer - a fear of that which is not understandable on the surface or relatable at first glance or is confrontive or provocative? Does that unexplainable energy threaten the viewer? Is it too unrestrained?

I think I challenge THE STORY. I have stepped outside the story to explore with no map. How can THAT be validated? THIS ART ON THE WALL STANDS ALONE WITHOUT THE NEED OF ANY OTHER STORY. This type of work will demand something from the viewer. It will challenge the fear. It will reveal the demons that point to angels, the suffering that points to joy, the darkness that points to light, the wounds that point to healing, the pain that points to ecstasy, the crucifix that points to victory, the soul that points to spirit, the earth that points to heaven. Perhaps the viewer finds this art too unsettling, too uncovering, too demanding.

No, a simple story to tell is all that is necessary, just a conversation piece.... a little color above the sofa. A pleasant design of color and shape will make everyone more comfortable, and the ego will not be threatened. The ego does not want something that speaks a language it does not understand. The ego needs containment, not something outside of its grasp. The ego wants structure, preservation, and mirroring of a contrived and established truth (even if it is not based in reality).

However, what speaks and uproots our own passion? Passion can be too scary and real, not like a horror movie where there is an agreed unreality (after all that's only a movie). This kind of passion can be considered "crazy" by societal rules but can also speak to a higher truth that is more sane than any other.

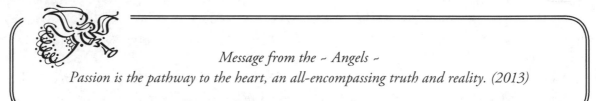

Message from the ~ Angels ~
Passion is the pathway to the heart, an all-encompassing truth and reality. (2013)

Mya always questioned whether Van Gogh was insane or had dark forces taking over his spirit. Was it the absinthe he drank, lack of food, lack of love and support? What finally was the last straw?

Could we say that the clarity in his paintings was undesirable because destruction was also present? Was the purity negated by an explanation of insanity? I don't know, but Van Gogh still speaks to me and many others across time, and the message has always been the same: intense passion and fervent love.

Mya is exhausted from experiencing the picture she has painted in her head as to the reason she has felt "invisible." But suddenly, she speculated as to what Van Gogh would think about people buying his work for the wrong reasons, and suddenly she had the answer to her own dilemma. IN THE END, ALL THAT REALLY MATTERED WAS THE WORK. THE APPROVALS OR DISAPPROVALS WERE ALL LIKE DUST IN THE WIND. WHAT WOULD SURVIVE WOULD BE THE WORK THAT WAS CREATED FOR THE AGES.

Message from The *~ Angels~*
The work is born in spirit and cannot be directed at will. (2013)

So it didn't matter, in a sense, how much money I got for my paintings or how many stories were told, even by me. I sensed a secret underneath all of it, a mystery buried by the sands of time and controlling Gods....Gods of greed, lust, bondage, and false prophesy. However, none of this has any power over the truth. One person, stepping forward and embracing freedom, hearing only one voice and speaking of and from love, becomes <u>THE TRUE VOICE BURIED IN THE RED MEAT OF EVERY HEART.</u>

CHAPTER 13

Where is the Love?

Where you go, I will follow.

March-99

Mya writes:

I sit in my new home in the Southwest staring out the window. I see a sprawling courtyard with grass and trees under a magical sky. I feel peaceful and serene. I feel like a hunted animal that has found a hole of safety – a hunted animal that has seen the last of its predators. I tell myself that all I have to do is catch my breath, and I will be fine. Doubts and apprehension penetrate as I question whether I am indeed safe. Maybe this is a sanitarium where peace is a bought commodity. Maybe I am safe, but crazy.

Suddenly I imagined Van Gogh leaning out of the window of the asylum, and remembered his letters about this period… how perhaps he also found some peace and relief. He had shelter and food, but most important of all he could rest and paint.

Her life the previous 6 years had been like walking through a minefield. She had had to face every fear imaginable. She wasn't sure she had survived. Every nerve ending had been shocked and every belief system threatened. But now she was safe. She had come to this place to paint. She had remained loyal to her dreams. She had come to the land that called to her and the destiny that awaited her, and she didn't care how many lifetimes were necessary to get her to this "now moment."

Of course Van Gogh was a part of her move, as he had been a part of everything for the last two years. She finally quit struggling with the synchronicities of their lives and sought to understand what her duty was — what she could do to ease the haunting — to ease the pain and perceived injustice. There was unfinished business. She was terrified of connecting with his spirit because of all the stories, but she had to go there, seeking peace.

⸺

I knew a little about shamanism and had successfully made some journeys into spirit. Of course, I questioned everything, but the journey offered me more contact with my inner truth than anything ever before, including my background in the teachings of the church. I wanted to know what haunted him and why I was feeling his unrest.

I set my intent in my sacred circle, called in my power animals, guides and teachers. I began to feel his spirit, his energy. I felt such heat in the left side of my brain - confusion. Behind my left eye - such pressure. I could not concentrate, focus. Everything was moving at such a fast pace. I wanted relief. I wanted everything to stop for a moment so that I could breathe in calmness.

I never felt out of control, just in touch with some other energy, but I decided I had enough information - so - I slowly came back to normal reality, amazed that I had gotten something so specific and yet so vague. I would be back to explore later. I was convinced that the answer for Van Gogh was also an answer for me.

August 2000

Mya was searching for clues through Van Gogh's life story. She looked at the period of impressionism in the art world. At some point, he became disillusioned with impressionism... that style of painting where dabs of paint attempted to give the impression of light. Her mind wandered, seeking to understand his frustration.

She saw him pacing, opening and clasping his fists back and forth, agitated about impressionism. He said, "Something is missing. The sun, yes, that is important and the light it produces, but the light absorbs all the colors and produces a distant reality. What about here and now - where are the soul colors and the colors of the emotions and the colors of the earth. I want a light that entices one into the mystery and colors that reflect the emotions, the feeling, the human experience. We are of the earth and of the stars.

For Mya, she wanted the same things, but she also craved a cool light... a light that had been blocked by the sun... a light she needed in order to heal - to create again. This light was not a searing, yellow, bright, intense heat, but a cool, blue light that was gentle and reassuring. BUT MYA SOUGHT THIS LIGHT IN THE DARKNESS. This light was hidden in the contours of the Heart and could be felt as emotion, and perhaps it was about the feminine, not the masculine.

Perhaps it was about the Mother - the energy that would teach her about THE HIGHEST LOVE: SELF-ACCEPTANCE.

So here in the Southwest, Van Gogh and I were beginning again, and we were hopeful of continuing on in spite of the fatigue and agitation and stress in the past.

I refer to the letters Vincent wrote, and I feel the gentleness and directness of his language. He said:

(1889) "I hope I have had just simply an artist's fit…."[10]

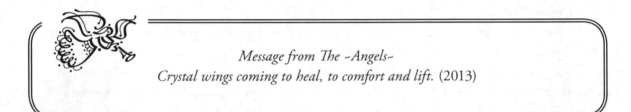

Message from The ~Angels~
Crystal wings coming to heal, to comfort and lift. (2013)

---

10 *The Complete Letters of Vincent van Gogh*, Vol III, p. 114.

CHAPTER 14

Making Contact

I am called by many names, but I always answer to the sound of
l o v e

What happened that day when Van Gogh died? And what happened that day Mya WANTED to die, but didn't?

Two and a half months had passed since Mya had her day of decision between life and death. Her lover had walked out the door, creating shock and disbelief. She questioned whether her experience with the sacred knife repeated Van Gogh's experience on his last day in the fields? Where were his angels?

Message from The ~ Angels ~
The angels were there in great numbers, and he did not die according to the stories told about him. He felt the presence of God and the angels, and he simply let go of his earthly struggle. He was enveloped with such love and such "holding" that his gaze turned toward heaven. He knew each ending was a beginning, and he was ready. (2013)

Perhaps the crows were trying to "caw" out to him, telling him there was another way. Regardless, on Mya's day of decision, there were guides and angels there, too, who patched together a shadow of what she had been, enabling her to walk through the life she had not exactly chosen. She knew there was healing to be done, but she couldn't look at the most vulnerable parts yet. So she buried the pain and used anger to slash her way through the routine of living, and picked up the pen to create a story. SHE HAD TO WRITE to prepare for her confrontation with those parts of herself that were buried.

Mya was familiar with shamanism; in fact, she had since recognized that what she experienced when she painted was closely associated with a definitions of a "shaman," one who entered an altered state in order to explore worlds and facilitate healing.

I knew that shamanism was ancient and that the shaman was both priest and doctor. In a PBS TV show "How Art Made the World," an episode called "The Day Pictures Were born" outlined theories of how the cave paintings 35,000 years ago came into being. It was suggested that these paintings came about because of sensory deprivation (extreme darkness in the depths of caves) and that a "trance state" produced powerful visions. Perhaps the emotional impact created a need to record or document or share the vision, and that these were simply "artists...nailing down their visions."... I believe these alternate states of consciousness were shamanic journeys, and I find it interesting that the motivation may have been more complex than researchers first suspected.

Somehow in our modern age, a lot of people are highly suspicious of such a journey, and yet we have traded in this natural ability or talent some have for bringing in "healing" for a healthcare system charging tremendous, outlandish prices for healing to a relatively few people. I think we need to re-examine the common use of the word, "cult." Perhaps our institutions have become "cults."

At any rate, without drugs or dependence on any other system other than the "Source," I journeyed with strong intent to remember who I was and who I had been. I began to remember lifetimes. Strangely enough, these lifetimes seemed always to involve being killed for who I was, whether I was Indian, holocaust fatality, accused witch, or Egyptian matriarch. I seemed to always have a secret. If I told, I was killed. If I didn't tell, I was killed. Perhaps these no-win situations caused my consciousness to regurgitate these situations until I could bring greater wisdom or insight to release angst. What was so dangerous about the truth?

For as long as I can remember, I WANTED TO MAKE A DIFFERENCE, TO LIVE A LIFE OF SERVICE, TO HEAL THE WOUNDS IN MYSELF AND OTHERS. And yet doubts always arose. The emotions of sorrow and rage emerged, regardless of intellectual rationalizations and theories. At first I began releasing these emotions, but soon realized they came from a bottomless well. What didn't erupt was converted into frozen lava deep in my center. I had to exercise some control, but always the question – where did these feelings originate? I had sought love, and found only heartache. I sought the truth, but found only isolation. I sought to know who I was, but only found countless other selves to be discovered. And underneath was a rage so vast I dared not go there. What right did I have to be angry that the world was not as I needed it to be. So I decided that If I had the power to create it with my thoughts, then I had the power to un-create it or tear it down and begin again.

Who were my demons? Why wouldn't they allow my intended vision to manifest?

My vision was made manifest in one place, my paintings. Each canvas was a battleground of good and evil, light and dark, love and fear. I fought well and hard. I found a deep satisfaction, confronting my fear time and time again! I triumphed, and after each victory would come a peace and an exhaustion. Rejuvenation followed each timeless war of the worlds; power gained from daring to dream, but for the most part I couldn't seem to maintain this rejuvenation and power for very long or rest in the peace of an attained victory. The aloneness would always return along with the magnitude of what I was confronting. I dearly loved my creations, but I wondered what they represented or symbolized. I knew I had to love myself and others to even attempt such a feat, but I questioned whether I was just "fucking" the wind?

⌇

She felt the futility Van Gogh must have felt on that "too hot" day… the crows attacking him as he tried to paint. The sun too hot – the darkness creeping into the blue sky. She was faced with the same decision – to give up - or surrender to something much greater. What was the difference? Was it possible to love too much or was she not loving enough? Love and fear and guilt. What was covering what? Did one mask uncover yet another? Who was she, really?

> *Message from The ~ Angels ~*
> *The mask was that of judge - both of you sentenced yourselves for a perceived failure. Your eyes could not see past the mask to the glory. There was nothing to forgive, yet you were unforgiving or sought an answer to a question that didn't exist. See beyond the "story" to the essence of truth. (2013)*

2000

Spirits are like impressions in light waves. If you know a certain spirit, you can reach them by tuning into a frequency. If Van Gogh could reach me, I knew I could reach him. I asked my power animals for protection and I set my intent. We needed to talk.

I visit Van Gogh in his room; he is sitting on the bed with his head hung low. I try to tell him of his success in my time. The news doesn't seem to penetrate, although I see a wavering of despondency. A question appears in his eyes as if he is saying, "Could this be true. Another time I find him at the sanitarium. "I have something I want to show you," *he says. He takes my hand and leads me into a garden – a beautiful lush garden. He comes to a rose bush and picks a particularly lovely pink rose.* "This is for you," *he says as he timidly tilts his head. Another time when I solicited his input, he said,* "I did the best I could." *When I asked what guidance he could give me, he responded,* "Love, and when you're done with loving, love some more."

Coming out of my reverie, I hear the song, <u>"Starry, starry night</u>," the song written about Vincent. I had always heard the song sung by a man, but this was a woman singing the words. I closed my eyes and tried to connect with Van Gogh, but he wasn't there. I sit quietly, and in a burst of energy I realized he was not separate from me. There was no "other," only us together. Every cell in my body vibrated to this truth.

CHAPTER 15

Fame/ Old Shoes/ New Shoes

Standing on the edge of darkness, I wonder if I want the light to hit my face.

What is fame? Mya shrinks from the question. Money and recognition and "earning a living" come to mind, but fear raises its ugly head. What will "they" expect of me? Will I have to paint what they want, or will I be able to paint what I am called to paint? Will "they" miss the point of the slashes of color across the canvas surface? Will "they" label, categorize, and "box in" my work to the point where I don't recognize what I have done and can't find my inspiration. My spirit needs to soar and be free. With fame, will I have to give up my freedom?

1878

Van Gogh's assessment of the situation was "to remain unknown and be counted for nothing."[11]

Message from The ~ angels ~
Fame is not always the answer. Your decisions cannot be contained
or stifled; they are registered in the ethers. (2013)

---

11 Vol. I, p. 151.

2000

What if Van Gogh's spirit had survived and was engaged in the present. How appropriate for him to gravitate toward a woman – the other side of his maleness… to continue seeking balance through opposites… to explore sacred geometry, the bones of the universe… to explore shamanism and sand paintings, the worlds of spirit and human DNA… to aid a mother and two sons, supporting their individuality and creativity above all else… to mother the new generation of wise souls… to give compassion to the abused and misunderstood. How appropriate that Van Gogh become en – "light" – ened to show how the light cannot be extinguished.

How appropriate for his spirit to come back and seek the spirituality and soul in a Southwestern landscape and sky… to come back to examine further the mysteries of light in a part of the world known for it's "light."… to come back, above all else, to see if the vision could be held without destroying self. To hold the beauty of the rose without being cut by the thorns, and to accept that there is no life without death and no death without life. How appropriate that Van Gogh choose Mya, to ban his grubby clothes (on occasion) for clothes that "make a statement"… to replace his abrupt manner with tact and diplomacy (on occasion)… to be able to prove the logic of his insanity and to extend his vision of the yellow house (a community of artists).

Mya could not help but marvel that her studio resided in a building reserved for artists, and that that building had been recently painted mustard yellow with lilac trim (the yellow house), and that new windows had been recently installed, looking out onto a street filled with the homeless. She also remembers being a part of an organization of artists banding together and coaching each other to overcome the obstacles of their "perceived stories." <u>One hundred and fifty years later, the dream continues</u>.

Mya remembered a photo of a painting she had done over 20 years ago. This painting was of a pair of old shoes. When she had gone to see a Van Gogh Exhibition 15 years later, she saw a Van Gogh rendition of almost the same composition. At the time she painted her "old shoes," she had not studied Vincent's life or his paintings in depth, and yet there they were, <u>two peas in a pod, or one pod in two peas</u>. She had to find that photo to reinforce her story. She searched everywhere for two weeks, not finding what she sought, afraid she wouldn't find it. She had a disturbing dream so she sought counsel with Kyalaka.

She had begun to think of Kyalaka in many forms… a higher self… an oversoul, if you will… a part of herself in another dimension… a future self… a dream self in a land of dreams outside space and time. Through her journeys, Mya went there, and she communed with her soul brothers and sisters.

Upon inquiring about the photo of the old shoes, Kyalaka said that I didn't want to find the photo because then I couldn't walk away from the truth and that I wasn't ready. Then she asked me, *"Mya, what are you angry about?"* I reply, "I'm angry that Van Gogh died. He had an appointment with greatness, and he walked away." *Kyalaka says, "You have to forgive Van Gogh for leaving. Let him go. You can't change history. It happened for a greater plan. You have to let Van Gogh rest. Don't you see – you are Van Gogh's redemption. There IS a happy ending. THE PHOTO OF THE OLD SHOES IS IN THE STUDIO, BUT WHEN ARE YOU GOING TO WALK IN YOUR NEW SHOES? The sunflowers are re-seeded, and you are the bloom. Celebrate! It is finished, Mya, look at the love around you – there is no tragedy, only in your eyes. Let Van Gogh die and live, not for him, but for you. You have the beauty of the sunrise – the calm after the storm. Accept the reality.*

I began to hear song after song on the radio that spoke to me of the search for love and self. I wondered what song spoke more succinctly to Van Gogh than any other, and what song would adequately describe my emotions today? I wondered what my new shoes would feel like, and if I could walk without falling down, if I could embrace the light, and if fame was in the picture. I marveled how these 20th Century songs spoke to me of days in the past, and how the lyrics were threads weaving through time.

CHAPTER 16

Nemesis

Forgiveness is giving to ourselves before, during, and after the fall.

August 2000

In re-reading my journals, I noted how many times I was given answers to my questions, but just couldn't seem to live the answers.

On one such occasion, I found myself being pulled back into the past, a past that involved a gun. I still felt the guilt creep in when I heard the gunshot ring in my ears. It was so final – so loud and yet so quiet. It was that door closing one more time – there was no turning back. The horror and panic of that was like being in the middle of a dark train tunnel, hearing the distant wail of a train whistle, knowing I didn't have time to exit the tunnel. I couldn't go back, and I couldn't go forward. I was caught in a moment where no decisions were available, no option, no way out. I also realized that I had spent lifetimes trying to change that moment. I had judged and punished myself AND VAN GOGH severely for being "human" - for not finding a way out. In response, I had tried to be superhuman. My lives had been spent in fear of that day when the door closed. I had now to pull myself out of that vacuum, that timeless space between the door closing and the door opening.

I had to accept fate and claim my destiny. I had to let Van Gogh rest and birth Mya. I had to trust the grace, mercy, and forgiveness visible in my life. I could not slap the Gods in the face by refusing their display of support, attention, and honoring. They had breathed life in my body again and breathed grace in every cell. I was faced with the greatest challenge of all – to accept life through death. There was a way out. I had made it through that dark train tunnel to the other side, and what I saw was "the garden." The garden with the "pink rose." The garden where guilt and remorse were not a part of the bounty and splendor of the Kingdom within and without. I smiled at the irony, the practical joke of the Gods, and felt my heart expand in appreciation and awe. Who said you can't go home again. I <u>was</u> home.

Journal entry: (2013)

If we do not share our wounds, we perpetuate them. If we hide that which causes us terror, suffering, and disbelief, we hide from the very divinity that would heal us. If we remain in our wounds, powerless as victims, we mock the very grandeur from which we came. Our disclosure of <u>vulnerability is our armor, our saving grace.</u>

CHAPTER 17

Robotic Interplay

...once you are Real, you can't be ugly, except to people who don't understand"...[12]

I smile as I contemplate how my past had healed, never quite in the way I anticipated. The past becomes the present only in those ways we (most of humanity) can incorporate all our experience by facing our nemesis – our need to punish ourselves for our perceived wrong decisions. We move on saying trite cliques such as "The past is gone - Living in the present moment is the key - The past is the devil's workshop," not having a clue about honoring the past. We have been brainwashed and filled with terror about cause and effect, karma, and Christian doomsday prophecies until we are frozen in a hellish moment, afraid to open or close a door.

Denial of our true selves allows us to live in the illusion of moving through time and space, taking care of the business of survival, if you will, while our hearts know we are dead – that we haven't awakened from the nightmare to the dream. Seeing thousands just like us living in this identity warp reinforces the illusion. If we see anyone that doesn't substantiate the nightmare, we call him or her crazy; we murder the threat; we cauterize the wound. No outside interference is tolerated because if one tear in the fabric of our illusion occurs, the infection of reality could take hold, and then the virus would wipe out humanity, as we know it. The robotic parts would be replaced with living tissue. The hardware would transform into true memory, and the programs run would support this true memory. Wars would cease because we would know the true enemy exists within ourselves.

In this age we are upgrading the illusion by putting microchips in people so that more control and manipulation can be possible. Our need to feel our connectedness with all life has driven us to false means to control life. More intelligence, more technology, more science, more – more – more! We are inheritors and dictators of planet earth, and we are drunk with power. How do you

---

12 *Velveteen Rabbit* by Margery Williams.

know what you are creating or destroying when you do not even know yourselves? The Oracle says, "Know Thyself." We try to prolong life at all costs. If you do not "Know Thyself," you are prolonging artificial life. Where is the seed essence of life? Is it in your cellular phones or your computers? Is it in your weapons of destruction?

You are creating in the dark. In spite of everything, the genome is being discovered, but do you think you will understand what it means if you see it before your very eyes. You take the truth and twist it for your own gratification. Wake up!!!!! You say your motivation is to cure disease and prolong life. Your medical science keeps people alive long after their spirits are gone. You know nothing about death, and yet you avoid it at all costs. What you consider "normal" or "healthy" is a survival that is disconnected from its source. You propose "family values" and the "American Way" and you are willing to murder, maim, and mutilate to support an ideal that is illusionary and rooted in insanity.

"Know Thyself" is not just a cute and trendy phrase. "Know Thyself" is the truth of your existence, a combination of the human with the divine. Do you want a world of metal when you can have a world of "light?" Does metal have heart and meaning? IF YOU GIVE UP YOUR HUMANNESS FOR SOME MISPERCEPTION OF GODNESS, YOU WILL LOSE BOTH. Your robots will be able to do everything except love. Your dream will be realized only to find the dream has turned into a nightmare. Wake up!!!!!!!!!!!!

Mya lived in this world of robots vs. "realness." She wasn't sure half the time whether her program was running from her own authenticity or from some headless monster who wanted her extinction. One thing she was sure of, she was tired of broken promises and rejection from galleries. She was definitely in the "upside down cross" syndrome, kept immobilized due to outside conditions. All she could feel in this moment was rage. How many sacrifices were needed to raise consciousness? Mya wanted to yell and scream, jump up and down and perhaps destroy something just to release some of the frustration she felt. She had no food in the house, no clean clothes; she had gone for days without enough to eat. She needed a cook and an agent. She needed money to insure some semblance of security. She had no health insurance and no nest egg. Did it always have to come down to this no matter how hard she worked, no matter how she tried to communicate or present her work. She came back to the moment when she almost took her life – "What's the point?" Did she pick an impossible task just to learn to endure suffering. That, frankly, was not good enough. Being a martyr left a bad taste in her mouth.

She wanted to taste the sweetness of life. She was tired to the bone of picking herself up after broken promises. She wanted someone to see her value and act accordingly. She wasn't greedy – she just wanted to be paid for the work she did or at least to have her physical needs met while she did it.

Journal: To much of the world, art is a luxury, not a necessity, but I saw things differently. Because of my experimenting with my life, I knew that art is "medicine," not just for artists but for everyone. More distinctly, COLOR HEALS. Art is the antidote to becoming a robotic society, the spare parts being materialism and capitalism.

The cat meows at the door. <u>The door opens and closes once again.</u>

CHAPTER 18

Rage

Rage against that which keeps you from the sacred mountain.

September-2000

~

I was reflecting on the insanity I saw around me. To me, the inconsistencies pointed to a culture of madness.

I wrote in my journal, venting and reaching for a higher frequency or some way that I might instigate change:

We, much of humanity, see enemies all around us, and yet we cannot recognize the enemy within. We are in fear of alien control that would contaminate our humanness, and yet we do not exercise that very humanness. We destroy everyday the very God we seek.

We punish ourselves everyday for some wrong imagined. We remain in ignorance because we cannot accept the truth. We rage against the elephant because SHE remembers. We rage against the world because we have lost our path. We rage against disease because we do not want to hear the messages of the soul. We rage against poverty because we do not want to see our impoverished nature. We rage against drugs because we do not want to see our own natural addictions. And most of all we rage against the darkness in ourselves because it makes us feel out of control. We must wake up and look at our rage - let it speak to us in the stillness of our own hearts.

RAGE IS SACRED IF IT SHOWS US THE ULTIMATE BETRAYAL. Rage is sacred if it shows us how outside interference has formed the life we thought we owned. Rage is sacred if it points to positive change. Rage expressed in the light of our own calling will prevent the violence in the outside world. We have a right to our rage. If we honor it in the appropriate way, we will reach the sacred mountain of our soul's dream. Rage against the Devil of Ego and embrace the angel of your soul's purpose. Rage, wake up, and dream another dream!!!!!!!!

Message from Archangel Michael (2014)

Rage is just passion thwarted. You have still not given yourself permission to embrace your passion. You are warring with your intellect and your "rules." Passion is not rational or connected to the ego. Once you quit trying to talk yourself out of it, the rage will transmute into passion.

CHAPTER 19

Why

Live with the right questions and the answers won't matter.

September 2000

Mya had many answers, and yet there seemed to be one question that demanded an answer for her to be complete. "Why?" None of the answers satisfied her – they were GOOD STORIES, but they had a contrived, tasteless quality to them. They made sense - they were logical, but they resounded with a dull ring in her ears.

Why did she paint? What was she trying to say? Why were her paintings so important and crucial to her life? Expression? Self-discovery? Truth? Sensuality? Beauty was essential – but beauty was all around her. She wanted to find the truth – but was it only a fragment of a larger truth? She wanted to face the pain and fear – but how many times must she open the wound? What was the wound? She had healed and transformed her life through her painting, but what was the gaping hole that remained unreachable? What had she traveled lifetimes to see, to touch, to feel?

She was the actor on stage standing on her hands, jumping through hoops, performing oratory miracles, crying tears of sorrow and joy, opening (on her terms) to receive the audience. Yet she was also the audience. She was the giver AND receiver, but still she heard the silence. The absence of response. "Mommy, look at me; I'm levitating. Isn't it dear? Be happy for me, Mommy." Silence. Again she was at the impasse. What was the face she was not revealing? What script did she hide under the couch? What was she afraid to portray? What mask was hidden from her eyes?

All she had learned and experienced was a bundle of discoveries, revelations, transformations, transmutations, transcendences, knowledge, wisdom, insight. And still her spirit constricted as she tenuously walked and talked along her earthly path, and her body responded with inflammation, pain, and stiff joints.

And love? What did it have to say? "You have not even touched the surface." The transcendence and focus yielded to more confusion and questioning.

As an artist, she knew that the nature of being an artist was seeped in not being satisfied, always seeking the "ideal."

Was she to be content with the search? Were her creations mere tracings of a vast multiverse of infinite possibilities? Maybe her creations needed no explanation or justification. Perhaps they were as Goya, the Spanish artist, said, "THEY ARE FOR MY SOUL: I HAD TO PAINT THEM." And yet was the search "to understand" to be abandoned because of its improbability? Or was she simply still looking for love and acceptance from those who could not give it?

She remembered a passage in the *Dune* series where someone is writing a letter to Vincent Van Gogh and saying that because of (him),... "he will not send useless love messages to ones who do not care."...[13]

Maybe she was looking for her true reality… the character she really wanted to play. What would happen if she emerged behind the cloud of non-acceptance and fear? What was she afraid to be?

She had often wondered why she had chosen to come into this lifetime because she never really felt that she belonged. She thought of Joseph Campbell's "Hero's Journey." What would the contribution be after she had completed her initiation, and would that contribution be scorned, ridiculed, or revered. In a light moment, she smiled and predicted that the responses would be ALL OF THE ABOVE… ha… and in this future moment, that was OK.

From little on, Mya was painfully shy, keeping her head down and failing to meet the gaze of others. She had her secret world that she kept buried within. One thing she knew for sure, she had to keep it safe. IF SHE DIDN'T, THE ONLY PART OF HER THAT WAS WORTH ANYTHING WOULD DIE. She remembered what had happened before when she had let her dream out of its cocoon.

She often dreamed through osmosis - sensing the dreams of others. Now she was dedicating her life to <u>her</u> dream, but sometimes this dream had no distinct form. It changed color as she changed and became more aware. What if the dream was what she wanted but not what she needed? And then there was always the intent to do what was for the highest good of all. She carried so many hearts in her body, and the irregular heartbeats confused her. When the hearts outside did not respond, she convinced herself she must concentrate on her own thoughts – that which was under her control – that of her own heartbeat, beating to the rhythm of her own soul. She hoped that intense self-reflection would lead to an intricate artery system connecting to all other hearts and to the pulse of the "God" heart. Sometimes she needed no food because she was feeding on the dream. She had to carry on to purify the dream – to create her map for the journey of her soul. SHE HAD TO LEARN TO RECEIVE STAR SHINE AS WELL AS SUNBURST.

---

13 *Chapterhouse* by Frank Herbert, p. 69.

Chapter 20

The Beginning

Sandcastles are lost kingdoms found.

Mya was 5 years old. Her home was located in a barren landscape – a dustbowl. Crops struggling in arid soil – winds howling and scattering sand to the Four Corners. She hated the wind and sand except when she sat under one of the few trees with her handmade sand-sifter. There she was safe. There she saw all the possibilities in the sand designs, the mountains and valleys of gravity. There she dreamed. Hours passed without notice, and her little hands were creating worlds. The colors had gone because she had to put them in a safe place, but she had the sand. She was the sand, shifting and falling and settling. This is where she felt love. She also felt love when Bonsai, her dog, greeted her with his soft fur and wet paws.

Mya was now 55 years old. She had long forgotten what she dreamed in that magic sand circle under the vast blue sky. She longed to know what her heart must remember about that womb of earth, that doorway between worlds. As she sat contemplating, she felt Kyalaka tugging at her sleeve. Evidently, Kyalaka had something to add:

"There is a land outside space and time where dreams are made. They are everywhere in some form or another. The air is pure and light. Here hearts are safe and joyful. There is one spirit and many manifestations. Nothing is bound to form; energy flows from one to the other. There is no scarcity, only an abundant energy that fills and nurtures every living thing. The rocks, trees, and plants are as alive as the beings that inhabit this dreamland. All is no less or no more than the sustaining energy that holds this dreamland in place. On the other side of this haven, earth, men have gone insane contemplating and remembering their loss. Others have forgotten. Still others have turned their backs, choosing for one reason or another to live in darkness. But the dream lives here in the ethers, ready to be picked up by some sensitive soul.

In the land of dreams, creation is effortless because the entire ecosystem supports the creative process. And what is the goal or end result? Joy… pure joy… that transcends fear, greed, and avarice. Hearts soar together as one; no egos, no guilt, no shame. No need for competition or struggle; only joy."

Mya looks at the words she has just written, and her tears mourn this kingdom lost, but her heart is also lifted as she resonates to such a vision. Has such a place existed throughout time? Perhaps, or maybe it only came into existence the moment Mya dreamed it, at least for her. She feels that Kyalaka, who helped her heal after her near suicide, resides in this magical land. She must keep the pathways open to travel to and from this land of infinite possibilities.

Mya clarifies her thoughts about dreams in her journal: she writes:

I feel that each of us must own our OWN dreams, or the dreams will be lost or wander the universe, never finding a home. Purgatory is a way station for these dreams. No one has the right to dream for another. Realization in one lifetime of all dreams is not necessary - what IS crucial is to incubate, feed, and evolve your dreams to claim your unique heritage. May all have the courage to dare to dream; the human race depends on it. Dreams are not static or one would be in perpetual sorrow; DREAMS ARE A RELATIONSHIP BETWEEN WHAT YOU KNOW AND WHAT YOU DON'T KNOW.

I, PERSONALLY, MUST FIND THE COLORS. I have some, but many are still hidden like colored eggs in a nest located in the land of dreams. I have to go there and retrieve these colored eggs to express all that I feel. Maybe I'll begin by sketching to free the lines, and those same lines will lead me to the colors. My studio is waiting like a patient lover, and Van Gogh still wants to paint. He believed that an artist's soul could be perceived in the lines and colors he used. I thought, "What a good way to be introduced to my "original" or "primitive" self.

Message from The ~ Angels ~
When you find colors that make your heart sing, you have found pieces of your soul. (2013)

CHAPTER 21

The Gospel of Freedom or Art for Heaven's Sake

Art should serve no master.

Art should serve no master. Art is free in the sense that man is free. Free will cannot be tainted with public demand, church dogma, government propaganda, or scientific methodology. Art to please "the church" is tempered by dogma, the patriarchy, and a distorted view of the history of man. Art to please logic and reason is to remove God from showing his face. Art to please the decorating and design trends of the day is to subject art to pure triviality. Art to please government or social agendas is to create an art distanced from a deeper reality of the nature of man. If an artist feels a calling, a higher purpose and/or entity will guide him. Because his calling is from another realm, he exposes himself to madness if he cannot follow the dream. He is outside mass consciousness; he cannot be otherwise. Although in essence he is serving humanity, he often suffers isolation in order to perform his duty. He has only the company of the Muse. This existence has its rewards, but it also has its pitfalls. How is he to live when society does not support his endeavor? Where does he get his food, shelter, and clothing? Where does he find a place to work? The priest has a parish; the judge has his court; the politician has his assembly; the doctor has his clinic; but all being paid to perform a service –

BUT WHO PAYS MOST ARTISTS CONSISTENTLY TO BE ARTISTS?

Playing devil's advocate, one might say that everyone has rules and regulations or restrictions on how they perform their jobs. True – but these jobs are all "in the system." The true nature of an artist is "outside the system." Such an artist is essential to "The Big Dream" and free will. Such an artist keeps the "human" in humanity. Such an artist can be a prophet, a seer, a sage.

Throughout history, except in ancient times, these individuals have been persecuted because they represent the power of the individual. Because of instances when this power has been abused, Hitler, for example, efforts were made to nullify any individual power claiming it was evil. (The witch hunts, McCarthy era, etc.) History has shown that man has extinguished every light that shone too bright out of fear and resistance to embrace the light. Martin Luther King, Gandhi, Joan of Arc and many others – they had a dream that threatened the illusion.

Once man turned away from the darkness in his own soul, he created enemies all around him. He sought knowledge in order to slay the enemy. Millions of dollars were spent in reinforcing this "new" technology. The more he tried to control and destroy the enemy, the more alienated he became with his own nature, and the more he sunk into materialism and competition. As a result, wars were abundant and poverty was rampant. Food (energy) was stockpiled. New devices of destruction, weaponry, and nuclear energy were invented. Extreme defenses were invented to protect a hullless ship. The façade had to be implemented at all costs. The truth could not be revealed – that there was nothing to defend. Appearances were everything – THE STORY HAD TO BE REINFORCED. No one life was indispensable. EVERYONE WAS FORCED TO LIVE THE SAME STORY OR DREAM. Individual dreams were destroyed to maintain the "story" created out of fear, greed, and corruption. Those who spoke out against this story were flayed, burned at the stake, tortured, murdered, starved, and ostracized. The crucial ingredient to maintaining "the story" was to kill individual dreams and memories. If they couldn't remember who they really were, then they could be led, coerced, and used to support the cause. However, if they remembered their innate power to create and control their destinies, then the "cause" was thwarted. Control was not possible. If the dreamers could remember, death would not be a threat because the dream was larger than life. Centuries of brainwashing ensued to create an army of memory-less robots.

And so here we are in the computer age. Man has discovered how to extend information to the masses, claiming empowerment and progression for the individual. But oftentimes, the knowledge has no face or soul. The individual has to discern amidst the overwhelming amount of information, but where along the way was he ever encouraged to form such skill? When had he been allowed to think for himself? What use is knowledge without wisdom? He had given up his right and responsibility to think for himself to the Church, State, and Society. He feared to take the responsibility of such an endeavor alone – so he gave that power to anyone who came along. Unfortunately, many who took the reign had no conscience or concern for the whole. The free thinker became an endangered species, and fear and control reigned over the land and sea. TRUE FREEDOM WAS NOT ONLY FOUND IN DREAMS.

The dreamers held the real world in place like in the Australian dreamtime. Otherwise, the illusion would remain forever. If a few souls did not dare to dream, the acid of illusion would have disintegrated the platelet called earth. Who were the dreamers – the musicians, the poets, philosophers, the dancers, the actors, the artist who heard the colors, saw the sounds, touched the mystery, and tasted the song of the heart and soul. These were the ESSENCE OF LIFE, no matter what circumstance. These were the only states that were above bondage – the only states that transcended duality and earthbound claws. But what does it mean to touch the dream? To open to the dream is not without its hazards. A strong will must be present; otherwise one is tempted to give up self to join the dream in totality.

CHAPTER 22

Michelangelo: The Shadow

We are but shadows on the earth seeking to know ourselves in the light.

Mya's birth name was Michelle Angelo. She had been incessantly teased about her name sounding like Michelangelo, the Italian sculptor and painter. She hated bearing that name because the shadow cast by such a "giant" loomed over her whole life. She seemed small to nonexistent in light of such a genius. She had gotten some relief taking her husband's name, but now that she was free, neither her given name nor her married name appealed to her. She had shortened Michelle to Mya and rarely used her last name. Maybe now she could find some peace. Now as she came to grips with her relationship with the Van Gogh soul, she began to project into the future to see what would come of the union.

She visioned a special exhibition in 2012 – the work of herself and Van Gogh. The vision goes thus:

I enter a circular room. In the center is a ring of crystals encircling a chair. I enter the circle and sit down. On my right is a pair of special glasses with lenses made out of titron. A voice says, "Relax, put on the glasses, and breathe energy into your heart." Suddenly a light appears above a Van Gogh painting and a holographic figure steps forward. "I am Ramus. I will be your guide. Welcome to the world of Mya – (Angelo) – Vincent. I look at the painting and a slight nausea sweeps over me as figures, strokes, and colors begin to move. The colors leave the painting and swirl around me. I am caught in the eye of the tornado. I cannot seem to remain centered or still amidst this hurricane of unexplained swirling. My only refuge is to look at the wall to the right of me – the wall dedicated to "Angelo" but blank. I am frantic switching from an awareness of the swirling colors and the blank wall. I am filled with terror – something is wrong. What is happening here? I can't endure this confusion. I tear off the glasses and run out of the room.

Afterwards, Mya sits, totally unnerved by this vision just when she was beginning to understand. NOW THIS!!!! She knew what was coming; she had to look at the shadow. Angelo, Angelo, Angelo

– what did it mean? She returned to her original name "Michelle Angelo"... a feminine version of Michelangelo. She felt something dark and ugly emerging, an unbearable sadness, a pent-up fury beyond words, and an unquenchable passion. Maybe her name was revealing a connection, a truth. She spent a day avoiding the disturbance she felt by immersing herself in television and nonreality. The emotion was too intense to deal with at this time. Regardless how much she tried to escape, the emotion surfaced as a sorrow, of unrequited passion.

She had woken up with the revelation of the futuristic connection of Mya/Van Gogh, and now she was plunged into a nightmare of uncompleted mania. She knew she had to look into a missing piece of the puzzle – Michelangelo. She grabbed her note cards from Art History in college and read the highlights of his life - creative furies, proud independence and daring innovation… exercise of artist's own authority… concrete realization of a intense feeling… partly finished figures that with superhuman effort, struggle to cast off the inanimate masses of stone that imprison them.

He seemed so tortured, so longing for salvation or desire for the heavenly realms that his eyes beheld a beauty rarely seen by others, a beauty that transported him to his source.[14]

Mya saw the commonality between Van Gogh and Michelangelo. Two men who answered to one call – two men whose work was interrupted, two men who struggled with religious persecution, two men who were familiar with "pent-up passion," two men who experienced "exile" because of their unwavering inward vision, two men who were seeking to make the soul visible.

Two men who painted things as they saw them (and felt them), not as they were, disdaining reality. Van Gogh wanted "his untruth to become more truthful than the literal truth," just as the Greeks wanted to create "super humans" rather than anatomically correct perfect humans.[15]

Mya was unsettled. What did it all mean? What was the core of all this intense suffering and struggle? "To be free" kept pulsing through her consciousness, and yet was Van Gogh, Michelangelo or Mya free, or did the longing only echo through the ages like bleating sheep lost in the hills, not able to find the green valleys of home?

By nightfall, Mya was stripped of any self-defense against this wave of emotion. She was not one person with a vision; she was many. She raged as one enemy took the forefront; the Church. She saw all the anguish of holy wars, of violence, injustice, and terror in the name of a "select" God. How many lives were extinguished because souls were not granted the freedom to explore God according to their own inner dictates. How does one fight mass agreement? Would there never be a heaven on earth?

As Mya journeyed to spirit, her hopelessness began to fade. In her own words: My guidance told me that creativity remains alive regardless of obstacles, and in the elusive "Heaven" or "Land of the Dreams, creativity was supported and "worked by a multitude of souls.

---

14 *Art Through the Ages*, Ninth Edition, p. 650.
15 *The Seekers: Gauguin, Van Gogh, and Cezanne* by Laurence and Elizabeth Hanson.

My guides instructed me to lie on my back and look up at the ceiling of the Sistine Chapel. A great calm came over me and a sense of celebration for such a creation. Look at the colors!!!! After all, in his own lifetime, Michelangelo became the archetype of the Supreme genius that transcends rules by making his own rules. His themes? CREATION, FALL, AND REDEMPTION.

I had my story, and the past had become my future. Michelangelo was the creation; Van Gogh was the Fall (or disintegration), and I was the Redemption (not in an egotistical sense, but proof that all was forgiven and that Michelangelo's concern for the fate of man was assured the powerful intervention of God and Heaven. I now had my 2012 Exhibition of Michelangelo – Vincent - Mya. Encompassed in the trio was a balance between male and female (the Mother/Father God), a tonic for despair, and a hope, survival, and reinforcement of art for the future. Also encompassed was the shadow: form/non-form, flying colors/frozen grey, and the salvation of despair. Connection, co-operation, and balance between and within should promise a "bright" future.

I remember something Vincent said about the two or three gathered together along with the Bible's verse of Matthew 18:20

"For where two or three are gathered together in my name, there am I in the midst of them." (King James Bible)

Vincent said, "**Blessed twilight, especially when two or three are together in harmony of mind and, like scribes, bring forth old and new things from their treasure.**"[16]

---

16 *The Complete Letters of Vincent van Gogh*, Vol I, p. 142.

CHAPTER 23

Religion vs. God

Love is a spiritual practice that transcends religion.

August 2000

Mya writes: "As a child I remember most vividly the need to be loved. I wasn't sure how love worked, so I tried different techniques seeking a "love connection" with another human being. I was relatively sure I felt love, but after that disclosure, the concept fell apart. What did it mean, this loving? I thought perhaps it had something to do with being good, but that concept was as shadowy as the 'love' one. And when I tried to be good or follow the religious ethics set down by my parents, I always fell short in some minute detail and was corrected. What did it mean to be bad, and how did I stop being bad? Guilt was born. I was told the only way 'to save myself' was to believe in Jesus and his salvation AND to go to church. But still the guilt was held over my head. I learned to mistrust every natural thought and desire, and I learned that my perceived shortcomings always surfaced time and time again. Even though Jesus promised forgiveness, I never felt "good enough." In the midst of religious training, "shame" entered the picture, and I suffered generational trapped emotions that seemed to be mixed with instructions for a Godly life. I didn't realize until later that this "shame" had nothing to do with God. This 'shame' could not be washed away; it always tainted everything in its wake. I could be humble, and in that humility was tenderness and acceptance, and God was there with me, but in shame, I was lost in some indescribable darkness.

But because I was a little girl with big questions surrounded by people who seemed to think they had the answers, I struggled inwardly having no one with which to discuss these feelings. Questioning religion was not encouraged or tolerated; so I stumbled along trying to be as 'good' as possible, to keep a 'lid' on the peace and harmony of my family. I didn't want to hurt my family; so the 'honest' love I sought was not to be found. In the midst of hugs and kisses, I often felt a sense that things were not as they appeared. There was a story underneath "the story."

Since as a child, my parents were like Gods or at least on God's side, I felt more shame having feelings that something was desperately wrong with this picture, and that a truth was being buried under niceties and a facade of righteousness.

These feelings colored every moment of life afterwards. Years of introspection and meditation followed. Years of trying to heal the wounds and alienation. Years of running away and ending up in the same place. Years of seeking love and finding conditions I could not fulfill. Years of trusting in the wrong people and suffering betrayal. Years of seeking the truth and my purpose for being here. Years of self-discovery, inspirations, and revelations. But as they say, "All roads lead to Rome."

As I healed and learned to trust myself and the knowing within, I adopted other kindred spirits into my "family.'" Still the hole in my heart for my original birth family was always there in the shadows. I felt a distancing from my original introduction to religion. I always felt invisible around those who held a narrow construct of who God was and what he wanted "his people" to do. Because of the certain religious dogma or a literal belief in the Bible or what they had been told the Bible "means," I was "excluded" because I didn't say the "right words" or profess the faith they had or "act" as if I didn't need "saving." I was never quite accepted or even seen for who I was, and if I was seen, then that seeing seemed to have an anxiety around it, a "worrying" spirit of fear. The sense or experience of love I felt always held a condition... an "only if" I accepted a certain belief. I felt "prayed over" - not in a positive way - but in a way that labeled me a victim or prayed over from a place of fear that I was misguided and needed to be saved. Neither assessment brought me any kind of resolution or peace. Why wasn't I "good enough" to speak directly to God, and why would God not speak to me directly in a language or "way" I could understand? And why would that have to be the same as another's, and why would I have to share that intimate relationship because of some belief or obligation to give testimony. Why would God need anything from me, especially if the story about the cross were true. My redemption and transcendence were my present, not only my future. Being stuck in the "crucifixion" story only relived the pain and suffering over and over instead of accepting the example with which Jesus gifted us - that we, too, can transcend and become one with our divinity.

When I tried to bridge the gap or explain how I felt, there was an uncomfortable silence. To please them, I would have to give up who I was and the spirituality I had found or lie to them, and I couldn't seem to do either. I was willing for the wall to come down, but how could it when their religious beliefs excluded me because I couldn't say the "proper" words or believe the words at the exclusion of all others.

Which brings me to the present. I wanted to be responsible and see the higher good in my dilemma... that my upbringing was exactly what I needed to find my path... to honor and acknowledge the different realities around me. But what was I trying to learn? What was the purpose behind the suffering?

Was the purpose to end the suffering or to realize that the suffering brought me closer to God and therefore was for my highest good? And in enduring the suffering, I would learn compassion and empathy for others? I would recognize those with the same wounds and embrace the higher love that had always been a driving force in my life? I would know that the battles through history fought between my God and your God were as meaningless as defending a truth that needed no defense? I would perceive of a God angry at humanity for insisting that their dreams were his, just as my parents insisted their dreams for me were mine??? I would face that living a dream not yours is a lie and requires the energy of lifetimes to maintain and defend? I would tire of a life not lived - a life not accepted by me because of honoring someone else's beliefs? I would learn about the land of dreams where one is free to dream without oppression, where love and support abound, and where one can be in the light of free will. I would be able to state my dream and intent, which is to enter the holiness of every moment free of any building, structure, or dogma – to enter the reality of my unique gifts and blessings, and to love as best as my soul remembers?

For that, I will endure earth's constriction and oppression and bless the oppression that reveals the chains of illusion that forces me to be clear with my redemption and the contract I had made with God. I can't live God's dream; I am only an expression of his Love. And When I fall from grace, I don't know if that very fall from grace clarifies another soul in his search for freedom and the truth. Van Gogh's perceived fall from grace certainly has been an inspiration for those whose hearts were open to the light, and Michelangelo would never have painted the Sistine Chapel if it were not for an oppressive Pope whose intentions were questionable, and Mya was proof of a redemption seeped in love and passion. Maybe God needs passionate souls willing to follow their dreams instead of robotic souls assuming to know the Will or Dream of God.

Her feelings of not belonging through the early years fueled her searching, and she questioned every belief, thereby allowing her to uncover who she really was - the diamond from the lump of coal. She was forced to stand alone and rely upon her spirit to see her through - the beliefs not defining or restricting her power to create herself, a being with a strength not depending on consensus or one version of the "truth." She would not have dug deep to get these treasures had she felt a part of the "tribe" in the beginning. Of course, this revelation dipped in and out of her reality as the pain and alienation lived on the surface. This discordance like the Pope in Michelangelo's case, were used to reveal the MASTERPIECE.

CHAPTER 24.

The Feminine / Masculine

She waits.

I remembered my own longing to be mothered by the divine and my disillusionment with the patriarchal church in which I was again "less than" and "under" the domination of the masculine with no equal partnership in sight. If the feminine was a part of God, why were females often rejected in societies? Why were their voices stilled? Why would there be a power struggle between male and female? Where was I in this archetypal soup? I was in a female body, which somehow was extremely relevant, and I had this overpowering need to create, no less masculine, in a sense, than Michelangelo or Van Gogh. I was menopausal and should not have had the instinctual procreation impulses, and yet I was birthing something in spirit as elemental as Michelangelo's figures of twisted muscle and straining spirit trapped in the solidity of pure marble.

Perhaps the feminine was the missing ingredient to release the "essence" from the stone (earth/womb) to join in union with the Divine Father creating the new race of man, the giants. What did Michelangelo's giants mean to him, and why did his figures have feminine properties as well as masculine? Did history need to combine the patriarchal with the matriarchal to create a "larger than life" race of humanity? Was this a dream of such magnitude that it surfaced in decade after decade in individuals capable of holding and expressing such a dream?

~

Mya felt such awe and reverence at such a "Grand Scheme." She was filled with humility and gratitude that she had been allowed to touch such an all-encompassing inclusive energy striving to be born. At the same time she was intimidated by the implications of letting go of the lie. Perhaps the birth would be stillborn, or maybe she would die in childbirth. She knew there would be pain as the dream pushed its way through the birth canal. Could She hold on – could she endure the eruption of energy pent up over thousands of years? Could she swallow the fear and tension spreading throughout her body of worlds? Would Spirit abandon her in her darkest hour, or would he be there to join hand in hand … in the responsibility of this child? And what of the darker forces who saw this birth as a threat to THEIR "Grand Scheme?"

She had no human contact that could offer her protection or loyal presence. In this – she felt alone. She was the single Mother with all the doubts and fears of taking care of her baby. She had all the financial and physical concerns and the distrust of the world's response to her creation. She was, after all, breaking the rules, which was necessary as an artist but also punished by the systems of a cultural society. She did not know if she could hold the dream under such circumstances, and yet this passion would not be still... would not be buried. She was caught in a boiling cauldron – ingredients not separate but combined and subjected to an alchemical fire transforming her lifetimes into a gestalt soup. Once at that boiling point, everything changes.

September 29, 2000

Mya had to get to the colors. They were prodding and beckoning. She felt so full and yet so empty. How would her newly acquired discoveries manifest themselves on canvas? What would the colors tell her? All she knew was that she had to paint. Interestingly enough, she found a discarded stretched canvas in the recycling bin that morning. Someone had released their attempt at a painted truth. Mya wondered why that attempt had been aborted. But here it was, and she grabbed the canvas almost guiltily, not quite believing she had been given such an obvious sign. She sat before the canvas forming her intent. She wanted the purity of Mya with the guidance of Van Gogh and the passion of Michelangelo. She wanted to build on their discoveries and wisdom. SHE WANTED EVERY STROKE TO CONTAIN HER ESSENCE AND TRUTH!

At the studio she gessoed over the colored images, and then she felt a stirring, an impulse so strong she had trouble waiting until the gesso dried. She made her usual division of space honoring the four directions in a cross and then she felt a circle slightly to the left of the center. Blue turquoise sky and Oh Yes – a sunflower! She declared her sacred circle, within which the highest good would reign and asked for her heart to be connected to the highest Light/Love, and prayed for balance of the masculine and feminine.

The passion impulse rose to such a crescendo that she could not even get the paint on the bristles of her brush but instead began stabbing the canvas with the end of her stirring stick. Turquoise slashes – four dark cardinal points – then the giant circle. From that point she began grabbing paint from the jars, and her fingers moved over the surface, short dabs and half blended circles. Picking up a brush, she graphically detailed strokes in white, yellow, bronze, and turquoise. Although she had a sunflower in the recesses of her mind, the stroked positions demanded a freedom apart from any subject. SHE WAS IN A STATE OF IRRATIONAL THOUGHT BUT IN A STATE OF PERFECT CLARITY.

She painted for two hours. Then she became quiet, strangely peaceful. She glanced at what she had done. There was no temperance, only energy!!! She was in shock at the Van Gogh strokes living in a dark metaphysical presence. There seemed to be too much of everything or an energy radiating out of control. She didn't understand but she felt some sort of completion or transitory resting place. She packed up and went home.

Everything was calm until night descended. As she crawled into bed, she was aware of being in a state of "not knowing what powerful forces were at work." She tried to go to sleep, but her heart was pounding in her throat. All night she was either too cold or too hot. The covers twisted and turned as her mind grappled with her soul. She couldn't seem to breathe. Where was the air???? She was suffocating under the pressure of some undiscovered truth demanding to be realized. The next day her body held unspeakable tension. The calm was definitely over. She was shaky and unsure what path she had taken — what deep dark forest had enclosed her. She sat down to write about the experience, but instead she wrote about her childhood and her feelings of "not being good enough." Although she came to a connection and conclusion regarding her, Van Gogh, and Michelangelo (regarding religious obstacles) she felt no peace. She knew there was more; SO SHE WAITED.

She ran errands and bought a cordless phone; which, strangely enough, seemed to be of utmost importance. Then with the anticipation of seeing a perceived finished canvas, she returned to the studio. As she opened the studio door and glanced at the canvas, she gasped. Oh my God!!! She became dizzy and was unable to "take it all in." The sunflower was not defined, and the subject and background merged in a wrestling match. The strokes were powerful, but they weren't grounded. Everything was flying. Mya found herself reaching for paint to end the agony as she hurriedly declared her sacred circle. SILVER – it needs silver over the turquoise. More yellow on the petals. Balance the roundness of the center of the circle. More red. Needs green. White/gold, red clay color. Mya was dancing a dance of balance, a walk on a tightrope. (She had to bring Mya's color sense in to neutralize the harshness). The painting needed gold and silver as desperately as a plant needs sun (masculine) and water (feminine). Suddenly Mya was aware of a softening, a gentleness, a joyous burst of growth freed from an ominous climate. When she stopped long enough to look, she was amazed at the transformation. THE PAINTING HAD AN EXTRAORDINARY ORDINARINESS.

Because of the iridescent gold, bronze and silver, the painting was interacting with the light and reflected dark as well as light. The silver (feminine) was essential to cool and incubate the hot aggressive energy of the sun (flower) (masculine). One could not exist without the other. The unrestrained energy was stilled. Man had found his woman, and woman had found her man. The union was one of peace and joy. Fury had found its maker, and the dream had found its dreamer. THE DOOR CLOSED.

Mya knew she was a soul that was determined to find THE LOVE THAT GLUES OPPOSITES TOGETHER, and she knew that the true form of this "union or <u>oneness</u>" came from the land of dreams. Mya was filled with reverence and privileged to have experienced this revelation!

I AM

the Angel of Balance and Harmony.

My wings stretch to enfold the "zen" of the moment, the exact preciseness of the coming together of elements to create serenity and peace and calm. My yellow circle is neutral, and the stones on the path lead to the in-between point of masculine and feminine, dark and light, and left brain/right brain. In this small place lies a complete universe waiting to be discovered. I open the door, but you must choose to enter. Blessings!!!

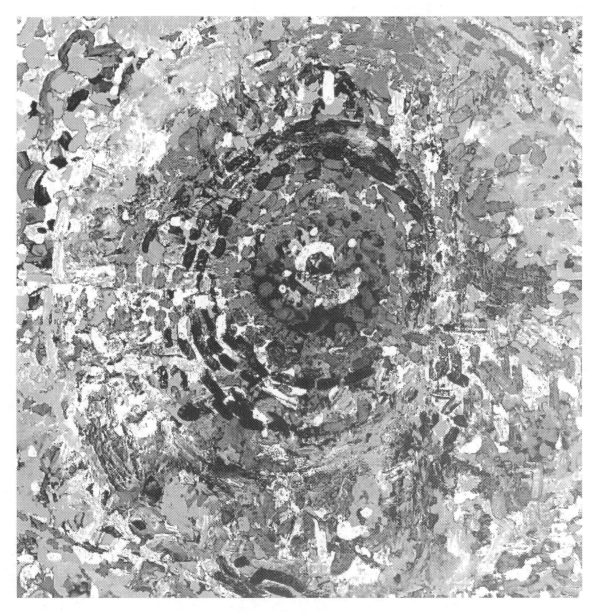

Van Gogh Circle

She had discovered the pot of gold under the rainbow – the bridge to the Land of Dreams, and she hoped that through her paintings and her painted words, others would find their way across the bridge to discover their own true form and intent. There were others who helped the Children of Earth to "see" and Mya rejoiced in this sisterhood and brotherhood.

When Mya tried to apply what she had learned in to "real life", she realized that the underlying theme was balance between male and female, not only inwardly in one person but outwardly in the patriarchal and matriarchal philosophies of societies, and even further into the balance within Spirit, God/Goddess. History resounded with accounts of woman, Eve, as being the temptress into evil or the "fall of man." With this story under the belt of humanity, man and woman alike were led to fortify themselves against the feminine. But was the Grand Scheme simply designed for man and woman to know themselves, to apply that knowledge, and to take responsibility for creating their own Garden of Eden in equal partnership? Debates as to who was created first, woman or man and why lead to hierarchical decisions as to which was more important completely leading away from the real question. How were they to be in relationship, and what was the goal beyond procreation?

She questioned whether humanity was to have a patriarchal society or a matriarchal society or an equal partnership? If God is learning through his creations as well as we are – then to freeze God's thought in patriarchal dominance or matriarchal dominance would be absurd.

Are we paying homage to the "shadow of God," a mere reflection of some fixed idea or reality? "Thou shalt not have any gods before ME." This commandment demands a God in the present, and if ME also includes us, then this God of Now is accessible within.

CHAPTER 25

Destiny/ Destination/ True Will

Our destiny is not a fixed point or destination, but an alignment with true purpose.

All this time Mya's destination was the studio and home. At the studio she stood before her canvases, emptying out to receive guidance and catharsis. Her trek to the studio involved being exposed to the disenfranchised, the homeless, and the mentally unstable. In this environment, she marched with her paint-splattered skirt up to unlock the door that separated her from the chaos outside. Out of fear, she kept the shades drawn, incubating herself in a cocoon of focus and determination.

She thought many times of Van Gogh's coal miners and laborers of the fields, many of whom probably felt some type of disenfranchisement or alienation to the world around them. Mya did not know all the stories of these people who seemed to have lost their way, and she could not judge them for their decisions or the lives they were living. All she could do was to receive all the guidance and clarity she could to unlock the door to her destiny.

However, she observed that often we, as humans, want to remain children with hard and fast clear-cut rules set up by parents. We do not want the responsibility of searching own hearts and minds for the obvious but ever-changing answers.

We would rather spend our energy fighting for our brand of the truth than to live lives of reality revealing an EVER-MOVING KALEIDOSCOPE OF GOD'S DESIGN. We would rather punish ourselves than live in the Light of Wisdom and Maturity. We would rather create illusionary enemies in order to have someone to blame for our own choice of darkness. What is within is much greater than that which has been created or projected because we have a ring-side seat to the panorama. By the time the experience reaches the outer limits, it is fraught with hearsay and dilution and misperception, along with infiltration of collective dreams. Why would God create a being in his own image if he did not insert an individual dream or purpose to be realized? Free will allows the dream to be disregarded, but True Will reflects the same Will as the Creator. How could it be anything else?

Mya was convinced that the definition of tainted Will was absorbing Wills or Dreams not your own. In a sense Will was free only as unrecognized uniqueness. To go against True Will was to choose Death or darkness of who you really are, and why would a being choose this death unless either they believed the lies or they willingly craved annihilation. And we ARE free to choose such a black void of nothingness. These individuals cannot be "saved" in the sense of rehabilitation or conversion. The natural state is darkness, rejection of True Will, and this rejection has a power to pull others into the same darkness.

In light of her reasoning and truth-seeking, Mya sought council with Kyalaka.

Mya: How can I use my Will to develop true understanding of what I need to heal, and to carry Love to a Higher Place?

Kyalaka: *What is called for now is a renewal of the faith that demands love in all forms – even Self-love – and above all, self-love.*

Mya: So what do I do now?

Kyalaka: *Do not reject yourself.....a martyr is not needed. LOVE YOURSELF!!! You are worthy, perfect, and redeemed. Go forth in Joy!*

Mya: I do want to when I get a small taste of the feeling, but I have trouble staying there.

Kyalaka: *I know. It's a hard one because you are on the earth's plane, and you still want to "pick up" the suffering. Know this – the suffering serves a purpose. Let go of trying to heal everything – your heart must not bleed itself dry. YOUR HEART IS FOR LOVING, NOT TAKING ON BURDENS. Let the Love and Light flow through Mya – don't hold on to it or analyze it – let it flow, and let the Creator handle the do's and don'ts and why's. He/she will not steer you wrong. We are so grateful for you and your Heart and your diligence, but, relax, you are protected in His/Her Love, and we want you to have a chance to PLAY.*

Mya: I want that, too.

Kyalaka: *And all of your family relations.*

I AM
the Angel who protects your growth,
your ability to dream, to envision, to play with Spirit. I help provide a nurturing environment
so that you can birth your potential. I hold you in a space of tender mercies allowing
you to have a safety net as you explore and begin to remember your soul's purpose.

CHAPTER 26

Old Forms Dissolving into New

Transformation

Picking up from Kyalaka's advice and information, I was comforted but still unclear as to the meaning of "play." I could not always stop the questions that popped in and out of my mind, like bubbles in a pond disturbing the glass-like surface... And there was that damn urgency feeling I had that would not let me rest ... not to mention all the synchronicities bombarding me daily. I began centering again on the idea of dreams and how they are born and the timing in which they decide to be realized.

I am sitting in front of the T.V. half watching, half dreaming, questions still running through my mind. I feel Van Gogh near as I get a shiver up my spine. He seems to be hovering over the mantle like a guardian.

I ask, "What was your dream and did you fulfill it?"

He laughs and says, "I am still fulfilling it. Art is a living, breathing organic pulse that is eternal. Why should it end when the body dies? Why should it cease to be relevant for only one space and time?"

He seems totally at peace now, not perceiving himself as a failure, being given an overview of his contribution and rewarded for his persistence in expressing the passion of his heart. He no longer carried the effects of the substances or the results of neglect. The tension is gone but the passion still intact. He is still smoking his pipe but with no ill effects... ha.

I looked at it as it had been before. For both Van Gogh and Michelangelo, a tense foreboding existed sensing some sort of fight ahead. Two souls caught in fear of a formless dread and anxiety. Two souls realizing that they were destroying the old form, following a dream that was only a faint glimmer. Van Gogh's colors flying with no single direction and Michelangelo's later figures imprisoned in stone. Freedom was the intent of both; old forms dissolving into new. They knew the dream needed refining, chiseling, and stroking. New vibrations were calling for changes and transformations. Van Gogh and Michelangelo would be back to play a new song that would be perceived by all the known and unknown senses. Their toil was not in vain.

Love was their paint, their marble, their clay. In these elements was born a new form, a new Love. Love or the lack of it was the driving force behind all their creations, and this Love brought Spirit to live in the Body of their Work. This Work was the laboratory of creation. Van Gogh compared the process to that of childbirth - pain comes first, and then a tremendous sense of joy follows.[17]

Dreams have to incubate, struggle through the canal, and then burst forth in joy and glory, and sometimes the Mother of these Dreams has to rest.

---

17 *The Complete Letters of Vincent van Gogh*, Vol. I, p. 204.

Chapter 27

The Gold Pebble

The Spirit Dream Realized

October 6, 2000

Mya was caught in this "redemption" aspect of the story. She had been told "she" was the redemption, but what did that mean? Michelangelo's "Judgement" painting haunted her, and Kyalaka kept asking her, "What did Van Gogh want?" As she struggled to "see" the implications, she was actually having trouble seeing with her physical eyes. Her usual prescription for contacts was not working. What had so drastically changed that she couldn't see in her usual way? Or maybe it was Spirit telling her to quit asking so many questions!

Mya, upon advice from Kyalaka, decided to try the projection into future once more, since Michelangelo had taken his place at the exhibition: Here is her account:

I open the door to a darkened room lit only by the light of the crystals in the center. I sit in the gold/ silver chair woven with the threads of time. I put on the Virtual Reality glasses. A green crystal appears in my hand, and when it touches my heart, I see before me "David" – Michelangelo's massive sculpture. It turns in space, and the hardness of the marble turns to softened flesh. It moves toward me and says, "You must slay the Giant." I become confused – how can I in my minuteness slay such a huge monstrous Being.? David smiles and looks at me with an all-knowing mischievous wink. "It's easy. Look at his weakness." But I ask, "How can such a being with such massive muscular strength be felled?" All of a sudden, a giant owl appears in the corner of the room. I can feel the softness of the feathers as they brush across my cheek. I shrink back at the magnitude of such a creature. The head seems to extend outside the room, and I am privileged only to gaze at the breast of this magnificent bird. "The truth – that is what you seek." I somehow want to bury my soul in its feathers of light and depth. I begin to lose the consciousness that I call my own. All that remains is a need to know about this confrontation between David and the Giant. Telepathically I receive the message – "Look at the giant's third eye!" I turn my gaze to face the giant. His eye was blazing, and I travel through the iris into a tunnel spiraling and cascading as a kaleidoscope of lights swirl around me. At this point I consider taking the glasses off, but then I declare, "By God, I paid for this ride, and I am going to see it through." I realize that my form has changed to a small pebble. "Oh my God, I am the stone that killed the giant…but who is this giant?" The multitude of lights combine in one golden light that surrounds and lifts me and gently brings me to rest on a pedestal inside a large cavern.

"Where am I?" I hear, "the gold field". "You are that which you killed. The giant is your rejected selves that are towering over you, threatening you with their size and power." I ask "What do I do now? I am virtually swallowed by the whale. How do I get out?" I look around this space and find Michelangelo slouched in a corner. He appears totally dejected and without hope. I speak to him. What can I do for you? He weakly turns to look at me not at all surprised to see me there. "I want so much for you to take me back to finish my work." "How can I do that?" I question. Instantly I find a gold pebble in my hand, and I know this is the way, the key out of wherever I am. "Take my hand", I say," we'll go back together." He smiles and pulls himself to his feet and leans on my shoulder. At the moment of his touch, we are transported in a flash back inside the feathery softness of the owl. Michelangelo's body is revitalized and rejuvenated.

He reaches out to touch his "David" and smiles. "Thank you – I have work to do – you will be my friend for all time. I have a gift for you." He hands me a bronze sword. "This is for you. With this sword you can slay any illusion that diminishes you." I am filled with some energy that I will name "love" and a connection to this giant of an artist I cannot name. I take off the glasses and the room is empty again, but with a green glow that I trace to the crystal still in my hand. I smile in peaceful bliss as I gently return the crystal to its place in the crystal ring around me. I rise and leave. The door closes.

I was a bit disoriented after this encounter. I visualized a sand-painting on an earthy floor, taking my hands and scattering the images and color, breaking the circle of experience, and thanking the spirits for their divine intervention. THE HEALING WAS COMPLETE.

Somehow, just as building blocks stack one upon the other, Mya was aware of her greatest fear: passion. She was still trying to keep a "lid" on emotion that she perceived as threatening to the "family" harmony. She was living a lie, trying to "paint pretty pictures" that would be acceptable to the Family of Earth. SHE WAS STILL LOOKING FOR LOVE AND DEVISING TECHNIQUES FOR GETTING IT. Even when she made grand efforts to be honest with what she felt, she tempered the portrayal with restraint and "holding back." SHE WAS AFRAID OF HER DARKEST HOUR AND HER MOST GLORIOUS MOMENT. She had pushed herself into hiding both afraid of revealing these to the public (or to herself) – afraid they would not accept or understand – afraid she would be met with disapproval for "going too far." And yet passion was not about control, but release. She had mistaken balance for control. Balance was possible between these two forces, dark and light, which was not about temperance, but about complete expression of both; THEREBY CREATING A PASSIONATE PEACE… a peace that was not dead and unmoving, but a peace filled with joyful celebration. How was this possible? She did not know, but the chain and lock on this door was "fear." SHE COULD NOT AVOID HER "PERFECTION" ANY MORE THAN HER "WOUNDEDNESS." BOTH WERE ANGELS. The lion could lay down with the lamb. The threat of extinction of one by the other was an illusion.

Something new had entered her blood and was coursing through her veins. To keep "order" at the expense of chaos was the game she played as a child trying to keep the "family" happy. Now something was spilling over. The soup was boiling. Hopefully the blend of flavors would be a delicacy… a nurturing, vitalizing blend of life force and unbridled passion.

She was the synthesis of Van Gogh and Michelangelo. She was David AND Goliath. She was Mother and Father. She was God and Goddess, and her creation, the child of invention, came from the womb of the mother and was born in Love. This child now had a life of its own – autonomous of both Mother and Father – free to create and Will its own destiny. The seed and soul had sprouted – THE SPIRIT DREAM REALIZED!

I felt the need to get out of my cocoon – out into the "real world." I dressed and went to my favorite Mexican food restaurant. I sat all alone in the smoking section. I had a twinge of longing as I watched groups of people and families managing their entrance, often stopping to help a handicapped or elderly member who moved slower than the rest. I thought of their plans to experience this moment together, and I was poignantly aware my plans began and ended with myself. In spite of all this, I relished the times spent in this section when I was the only customer. Somehow I could more intensely enjoy the sensations of eating without the possibility of being watched. I could savor each smell, taste, and flavor.

Although complete, my senses began to wander as I watched the intimacy or lack of intimacy in the gestures of others. The weather had turned cold, and I longed to touch another for warmth and consolation… to explore a body outside of my own. I remembered my last short-lived relationship or "romance." But then again, I had my work.

CHAPTER 28

Money

Money is "manna".

Mya writes:

Anger rises as I reflect on the way Michelangelo and Van Gogh had to "beg" for money to continue their work. What, if any in their personalities, disallowed receiving money? Did they hear from their time the same adage I heard from my time, "Money is the root of all evil.?" Kyalaka interjects: *"Money is not the root of all evil; greed is."* When Van Gogh and Michelangelo did not receive money for services rendered, they continued to "push forward" in spite of the lack for needed resources.

However, I am here, and I want to do what I came here to do. Is such a gift to be kept in shadow locked away in a studio lab, or does that gift deserve to be seen by the inhabitants of the earth plane on which it was created. If the creations came from the Land of the Dreams, are they created only for that Land, or are they destined also for the Land Below. Am I not to consider my work mine and expect payment? I scream out to the Heavens: I am ready to receive. Unlock the door to receptivity and abundance. I am worthy. What unspeakable malady punishes me? How many lifetimes does one choose to be in such frustration? What purpose does it serve?

I am willing to endure if there is a solution, but I feel as if I am a toy of some sadistic principle that refuses to allow me to have the very bread of life. Let me out of this dungeon. Let my heart release if I am creating such a barren landscape. Let me taste the nectar and feel the lushness of the green vinery of the jungle. Remove these chains I have created. RELEASE MY ESSENCE FROM THE STONE. (Michelangelo) Giving, giving, giving with no love that would receive. Chipping away from inside the mountain trying to reach the surface to see the meadow. My soul longs and aches.

If there are no injustices, then help me rise above my self-inflicted prison. I believe in grace and mercy – give me the power to slip through the barbed wire fence to reach the path outside. (The barbed wire fence was an image that Mya saw in many lifetimes). Let me out!!!! How could you do this to me? Can't you understand what this is doing to me? What have I done to warrant such treatment? Let me out!!!!!!

If God implanted me with this desire to paint, and I do then, why doesn't he use the paintings? Am I to work on a Grand Plan of which I have no clue? Who is picking up on my creations? What are they but essences trapped in stone? Why? If they are only to refine my soul, then what do I do with this body in earth's dimension? Why am I here?

I'm perfectly happy when I consider only myself, but I come time and time against the fact that I am part of a globe, a country, and a community. Where do I fit in the larger picture, the one that roots me in the Now present ground. What do you want of me?

I admit my faith is weak, but I keep hoping, unable to attach myself to a plan unseen. I take step after step on faith, but I come back to my knees when I fail to "see." If I'm not seeing the signs, open my eyes and heart. The dreams last night destroyed the inspirational signs I felt yesterday. Is this the dark side trying to extinguish my light? Kyalaka interjects, *"Yes."*

I close my eyes, and Vincent is there, comforting. He soothingly says, *"There is a plan, a Divine Plan. You are doing great; gather your strength and fortitude - the best is yet to come."* I smile as his words seem like a conglomeration of platitudes, but then I reach down and really *"hear"* the surety in his voice. He ended by saying, *"Be true to yourself, and everything will work for the Highest Good. Your 'harvest time' is coming."* Love, Vincent

CHAPTER 29

We are All One

The Key of Life - the Divine Feminine

OCTOBER 15, 2000

I took my sketch book and began "pulling in" Michelangelo. His face was angry, disappointed, frustrated. It bears the marks of defeat. What was I to do with this? I knew I had to raise all the emotions to a higher octave, to not deny the emotions but to love more to bring them into another environment, to not fix them, but to allow them even more passion. I DIDN'T KNOW WHERE I WAS GOING, BUT I KNEW HOW TO GET THERE. Van Gogh and Michelangelo had made their contribution, but I had now been handed the ball. I felt an overwhelming sense of responsibility to win the game for the team. Somehow I would know what to do. Somehow I had to not think my way through, but feel the action I must take. The adrenaline was flowing, and anything was possible. I had found my uniform and number and field on which to perform what I had been coached to do outside of space and time. As in battle, I was experiencing time in a dance of motions thrust on me with no turning back. I was a pawn in the game of life, and I knew I had spent lifetimes getting to this one pregnant moment.

OCTOBER 29, 2000

Mya looked at her name. With an "a" added, it became "Maya" which was illusion in Eastern thought. Was she an illusion? In some way she felt exactly that with Van Gogh and Michelangelo's dreams coursing through her veins. She felt so small and distant as if her dreams were small compared to these giants, and yet she knew she had the same potential; otherwise, their dreams would not have awakened her. SHE HAD SEEN THEIR DREAMS THROUGH HER EYES, BUT HAD SHE SEEN HER DREAMS THROUGH THEIR EYES?

JOURNAL:

I was attending an artist workshop in Sedona, and we were assigned a special project. We were asked to dress in costumes and make masks from supplies scattered over many tables. Since we had been working with the power of language to create and transcend the stories of the past, we were asked to stand before everyone and declare who we are and what we wanted to say.

I, of course, chose Van Gogh. I decorated a mask and wore a silver cape. We hid behind a screen to make our entrance. As I stood there, my heart was pounding. What would I say? What voice would I hear coming out of my mouth?

I walked out and viewed the people waiting to hear from me. It was surreal. I paced nervously with my head down and arms outstretched, fists continually tightening and releasing their grip. I felt such agitated passion as I spoke as Van Gogh:

"Mya, Mya, Mya. How can I express what Mya means to me? How can I tell the world what she has dared to do? She dug up my sketch out of the sands of time, added the colors of the universe, added the colors of her heart, and continues the dream. She is my child, my mother (voice catching with emotion) and my lover. WE ARE ALL ONE."

He swings around in a sweeping motion addressing the 21ˢᵗ Century souls – "WE ARE ALL ONE – do you hear me – ONE! Mya opens the door for all of you – it is a gift she gives at great expense to herself. In spite of this or because of it, Mya is finding joy and peace. She, I, we are victorious. You, the world of now, need to know this possibility of triumph. Mya shows you the proof, the absolute evidence, of this fact. We do not die; we continue to create. With this knowledge, time and space do not restrain you in this ability to act, to create, to make known the unknowable."

Later I felt Van Gogh speaking privately to me, saying that he was passionately indebted to me for listening through time to the voice of reason and non-reason, and looking in my heart for the compassion to reinterpret and reinvent spirit and soul. "The world may never discover what you have done," he said, "but I want you to know that I know, and even if that recognition remains a secret – oh, what a marvelous secret. Many have died for less."

I could hardly take in the words. The words came not from my present myopic view of my circumstances, but from a powerful presence making its entrance through the mask in response to my stand, no matter how timidly made.

Afterwards, everyone was stunned by my performance: we all were a bit taken aback and wondering what we had just witnessed. People came up to me and said, "Wow, that was powerful!." Later many came up to me as I was leaving the workshop, saying, "Leave Van Gogh behind - move on, move forward."

I understood their comments to a certain degree, not really understanding what insight or revelation had come to THEM, but I wasn't prepared or felt it necessary to leave behind this integral part of who I was.

The validation from Van Gogh and my friends was going to take time to receive. Interestingly enough, SUCCESS WAS AS DIFFICULT TO TAKE AS REJECTION. BOTH REQUIRED A RE-STRUCTURING OF VIEW OF SELF. And yet true success would be achieved when neither would affect one single hair on my head. And I knew that that state of mind was what I sought. All the fear of success/failure was based on the ability to be influenced by outside opinions. ONE DID NOT "HANDLE" SUCCESS OR FAILURE - ONE STOOD IN THE CALM CENTER OF THE HURRICANE OF BOTH. That was freedom! That was the Abiquiu of Georgia O'Keefe and the Sistine Chapel of Michelangelo and the Wheat fields of Van Gogh. How simple, yet how difficult to maintain or even touch.

OCTOBER 30, 2000

Mya felt she was drawing "like souls" around her like a mother swan protectively draws her ducklings under her wing. White feathers can show the way to the sacred mountain. She questioned her ability to do such a momentous task, but she knew her destiny demanded it of her or rather gave her the opportunity to do so. When she embraced the notion, she felt calm and at peace as if she had finally found her heart's wish. Not only that, but that she was the bearer of a secret so deep and mysterious that centuries had buried it within the bowels of the earth itself. Was this the time for the secret to be revealed, and what was it? Was there risk in the telling of such a secret? What would be the forces that would try to keep it buried? Mya shivered as the implications spiraled through her body. Did she have the Courage? And yet she knew her life was only a shadow if she shrunk from the possibility. What did the solitude reveal to O'Keefe, to Goya, to Michelangelo, to Van Gogh. WHAT DID THEY DISCOVER IN THAT PLACE BETWEEN THE DOOR OPENING AND CLOSING?

JOURNAL

I knew death was a player – O'Keefe's bones, Van Gogh's reaper, Michelangelo's Last Judgment, Goya's demons/angels. What was still to be revealed about their vision? I felt an urgency that would not let me rest. WAS I AFRAID OF DEATH OR AFRAID I WOULDN'T DISCOVER WHAT WOULD ENABLE ME TO SURRENDER TO LIFE? What was this reservation – this tension that I must be aware every second lest I fall prey to ignorance, to deception? Was this what life is – a constant vigil?… a vigil that isolates and protects. What balance is necessary to hold such energy? Whatever it was had to be IN THE BODY, not just spirit. I felt that all the rejected parts were demanding to be seen in the light, in the body of THE FEMININE.

The feminine was not gender related but a state of consciousness. In an age where patriarchy dominated and burned, civilization was breaking down in a spasm of birth pangs. The searing heat of the masculine had to be cooled by the feminine, or earth would explode in a reign of hot lava and spasmodic convulsions. The Mother had to be given her place in creation. Her name was part of the totality of God, and she could no longer be ignored or blamed for the sins of the world. SHE ALONE HAD THE KEY, AND IT WAS THE KEY OF LIFE!

CHAPTER 30

Light

Light attracts that which desires to be seen.

JOURNAL:

I was always struggling with the light. I had bought into the notion that in order to paint, one must have the "right" light. I had filed through hundreds of theories about florescent light, north light, warm and cool light, etc. etc. I had painted in rooms with skylights, rooms with one small window, rooms with windows from every direction, and even rooms with only a spotlight. I still struggled. Even with adequate light, the easel had to be placed where my body did not cast a shadow on my work, which even narrowed the possibilities further. Not only were shadows a problem but also glare. The problems were endless. I now had good windows in my studio with tract lighting AND florescent lighting. And what did I do? – drape the windows and turn off the florescent light and paint only by tract lighting. Even still I painted more effectively at night when the light coming in the top windows was no more. I even painted with my eyes half closed to cut out even more light. Finally I realized I really didn't paint with my eyes but with <u>my instincts. </u>I didn't see visually; I felt telepathically. I essentially was going into the darkness to bring out light; therefore, I had to narrow my focus and eliminate outside stimuli. I wondered sometimes whether going into that constricted visual and paying attention to whatever glimmer of light I found made that light brighter. What if attention equaled love of some kind, and that love changed the recipient in some mysterious way – brought more light to its essence. If this were true, then WHATEVER WE LOVE OR PAY ATTENTION TO OR OBSERVE BECOMES "LIGHTER."

This was all very well and good, but I had to consider the lighting in rooms my work would be displayed. I also observed that most people were drawn to "light" paintings rather than dark ones, but at the same time, I was a colorist and light diluted color. I also knew there was something underlying this study of light that I had not discovered yet.

I then began reflecting on the light conditions of the past - the sun, candles, oil lamps. What of Michelangelo? What light hit his retina or soul lying on his back with paint falling in his eyes? How could one obtain any consistency with changing light? What looks glorious outside; inside becomes dark and muddy. What was it about light itself that complicated the issue?

"Light travels in circles" was a message I had received when inquiring to spirit about this complex issue. As often with Spirit, it was up to me to figure out the details. Normally, one would think of light traveling in a linear beam from one source to another, but what of this circular light? I thought of the swirls around planets and stars in Van Gogh's paintings. I thought of Michelangelo's insistence upon changing a wall so that the top curved forward. I thought of the difficulty of using circles in my paintings because, in essence, the circle is complete within itself. I thought of the flickering movement of a candle flame. If light moved in circular pathways, then EVERYTHING HAD ITS OWN SPIRAL ENERGY, GOING FROM THE OUTER EDGE TO THE CENTER AND FROM THE CENTER OUT AGAIN.

Perhaps light was closely related to time. Michelangelo's figures twisted and turned in time even to the point that some figures were displayed basically both "coming" and "going" – and both going up and going down. From where had Michelangelo's design ascended or descended, and why was he so insistent upon having complete control over its implementation? And why was the design to this day a mystery and fraught with hidden meanings? And what, if any, meanings were revealed based on his color choices? There was a secret here if only the light was "right." And if light was knowledge, then perhaps finding it was "accessible." And if that light traveled in a larger circle, it could be possible that it would return with more light or knowledge from some unknown source. AND IF COLOR IS A PARTICULAR RAY OF LIGHT; THAT COLOR COULD INDICATE ITS SOURCE.

A perspective tool was used in the past to find the vanishing point. Was that vanishing point the center of a larger circle? And what of our clocks, hands traveling in a clockwise fashion around the circle with the pivot in the center. Was it possible to reverse or go back in time if the hands were propelled counter clockwise? And if so, then the past and present were parts of some simultaneous whole depending on where the light was or how it was bouncing off of objects enclosed in the circle of time.

The Egyptians, I believe, knew the answers. Gold and copper were used on the masks of their mummies, and we do not know what effect these minerals had on time, but a display of wealth was not the only factor. All metallic surfaces catch the light and maybe bend the light or refract the light changing time itself. Why did some pyramids have gold capstones? Why was gold valued in primitive cultures above and beyond the monetary value?

I was driven to learn the secrets of light. I had explored metallic paints, and I knew that the changes made in the painting as light traveled across these surfaces was not only intriguing but revealed some universal metaphysical property. The answers were linked to the Egyptians and other cultures before and after them, but these answers were kept as secrets for a reason. Light is knowledge, and knowledge is power, and power is hoarded for inclusive reasons.

CHAPTER 31

The Mother

At the age when the mother loses her first major soul part, she mistakenly captures her child's as a replacement.

Sometimes a mother and daughter are too close or too distant for healthy bonding. If they are very, very different, a discordant relationship can develop - the distance too great for mutual understanding, and total acceptance of the other is next to impossible. For whatever reason, I felt I was seen as a projection or as a mirage of expectations and assumptions. This was very painful and debilitating causing me to either pretend to be the expectation or be rebellious and belligerent, or withdraw into depression. Under the umbrella of love, I felt rejected and invisible. However, in my paintings, I portrayed the Mother/child archetype repeatedly, and I realized this expression provided a satisfaction to a need I had no other way of fulfilling.

I always became one with my creations, and the creations brought me a broader knowledge; perhaps it was being in touch with magic or expansiveness or the power of an archetype. Whatever, I found that when negativity or need arose, Spirit provided a way to reach the positive. HELPING ANGELS, SO TO SPEAK. So, in a sense, because of my feeling of a lack of support, I was driven to channel or create the opposite in my paintings. I discovered my spirit in the paintings, and my paintings spirited or fueled me even when I expressed the pain OR because I expressed the pain. Spirit tricked me by luring me into the colors, and the colors anesthetized me to continue the journey. If others did not respond to my paintings, I frustratedly felt like screaming, "Don't you see – don't you see the miracle. You, too, can have this miracle. You, too, can experience this dichotomy."

And the first time I touched the power, I wanted to share the importance with the world. How many lives could be changed from hopeless desperation to awe and marvel at what was available, at what was possible if they only OPENED THE DOOR. I felt I had been given a gift, but the gift was not a "talent" per se, but A WILL AND DETERMINATION AND OBSESSION TO TRANSMUTE THE POISON AND TO TRANSCEND.

CHAPTER 32

Two Masters

Who is this "I" that is here, and who is this "us" that is everywhere.

NOVEMBER 9-2000

Mya woke after dreamtime remembering something about traveling through tunnels and seeing images – pulsating strokes mapping out black trees against maroon skies. Strokes gave way to blue pinpoints of light extending up and away into a cosmic heaven. Instead of a rapid fleeting impression, the images remained as if to say, "I am here." She was relaxed enough to not let fear scoot the clarity away. She was remembering. She was allowing the truth to make itself known. She was surrendering to her destiny, to the divine plan, and she was ecstatically happy. The reality was breaking through her waking dream. She had a sign that the nightmare would end, and that the door was not locked shut and that her previous "funk" would give way to inspiration once again.

JOURNAL:

Strokes flying, masses of grey-green, twisting spirals, and joyful sorrow. Impermanence of life frozen in one moment to be forever captured so as not to ever forget the essence of felt memories. The smell of coffee, the awakening to a new day when the format has to be remembered but the format is gone and has to be reinvented. When each day is greeted as if there are thousands of yesterdays, but no past – as if there are thousands of selves – but the challenge is birthing a new self – when nothing is sure – but everything is possible. When the heat of the sun demands the cooling shadows and my heart aches for its other. When the cat meows yet again at the door and the body makes the same monotonous motion to open the door. What if the body refused. Then I suppose the body would have to ignore the cat meowing at the door. I couldn't ignore that sound disrupting my peace. And yet sometimes I felt exasperation letting the cat in, knowing the demand for the same action would be repeated (probably in 5 minutes). What was the sense of all this coming and going?

I felt that the Van Gogh inspiration brought purpose to my life, but at the same time, I was dealing consciously with the challenge of bringing together many lives in some array of shape and color. I wasn't sure anymore there was just an isolated Mya identity without the other voices. That perception of a single "I" was gone. But when the impressions and connections with Van Gogh faded, I felt lost and undirected.

The routine of living was tasteless without the assurance I was on a mission, working under the umbrella of something magnificent. When the clarity of that "something" faded, I was the cat meowing at the door. I was a shadow aimlessly walking through space. I was small. THE WORLD CARED ABOUT THE VAN GOGH THAT WAS SUPPOSEDLY DEAD, BUT I WAS UNRECOGNIZED AND INVISIBLE.

I was well aware what the psychologists would do with that admittance. They would say I was suffering from grandiose personality or schizophrenia, but I knew I was looking for the truth, a meaning to my life in a meaningless world. What did I owe this lifetime apart from any knowledge of the past? The knowledge was a double-edged sword. Being immersed in the Van Gogh lifetime, I was serving two lovers or two masters.

CHAPTER 33

White Eagle

She who walks in beauty.

I felt the disturbing feeling that more was surfacing, perhaps another lifetime. Why had I come to this location on the planet? I remembered walking among the Indian ruins, hearing the voices of the ancients calling my name. I was not interested in the "Savior" concept; I just wanted to honor my heritage – to benefit from the knowledge and treasures of the past in an effort to be as responsive as I could to my true nature. Flashes of village life, of home and family, of Indian ancestry. I could smell the campfire and hear the sounds of Indian life enveloping me like a warm blanket. Strangely enough this Indian life and Van Gogh's spirit seemed to be connected. As I let these words sink in, my body shivered with recognition.

Sometimes I yearned for nothing to have meaning beyond simply being. I loved the searching and the revelations and insights, but as with everything else, they faded or demanded the next step. I wanted to be in touch with life between the DOOR OPENING AND THE DOOR CLOSING. I needed to be beyond linear time. I needed to be IN THE CIRCLE OF TIME in where Van Gogh, Mya, and all the others were one complete whole, not experienced as one fragment after another. The strokes had to be overlapped, building a base, a structure, where all could exist SIMULTANEOUSLY. The colors were not isolated into dark and light, but all colors were together forming layers of time building up until the immediate present. Then and only then could I feel as if I were beginning with what I needed to create, the OBJECT OF MY DESIRE.

I knew that Eagle was my power animal in many of my Indian lives, and now that power seemed to want to help me now. Eagle would help me see the overview from above, the patterns of the landscape of my mind. With the help of his powerful wings lifting me effortlessly on the wings of my spirit, I felt my power return, the energy of my life force, my strength. The surge was immediate and all encompassing. Eagle was spreading his talons to swoop down on the food that would sustain my life. I could see through Eagle's eyes to spot opportunity from a distance because

97

Eagle had his eye on the center, on the horizon. Through Eagle, I could work with that which was above and that which was below to navigate my flight.

I flashed on journey after journey where I had been given a white Eagle feather. The feather marked a recognition by Spirit of accomplishments and acknowledgment of lessons learned and levels reached. I trusted Eagle now to tell me what was needed and what had to be left behind. My mission was to build trust that I would be shown the way to endure by grounding the truth and making peace with my flight. I looked out the window – a dust storm of snow began to swirl in Van Gogh circles, EACH SNOWFLAKE TAKING ITS OWN DIRECTION WITHIN THE CIRCLES.

November-2000

JOURNAL

I struggle to get food in my stomach, to feed the cat, find warm clothes, and make my trek to the studio. Artistically, what discoveries were mine, and which ones were from Van Gogh? I must be me with Van Gogh revelations, not Van Gogh with my hand. I felt no inclination to copy or replicate. I could do that easily enough. I needed some assurance that the Van Gogh ability was there, but I needed to incorporate it with my own artistic vision. I declared my stand to act from this point of reference. In the middle of this declaration comes an overwhelming fear that I would be successful in touching this energy, and, at the same time, that I would fail to touch it.

The energy sneaks in my drawings when I am BETWEEN THE DOOR OPENING AND CLOSING, THE MULTIDIMENSIONAL GAP. Usually, it lasts only a few minutes when my conscious mind is at rest. Then as the thoughts return, I am filled with fear that such "letting go" could overtake me or trap me in a dark place. Fear could close everything down, or I could inch out and explore a bit to check out the feeling tone - to trust that I was here in this place and frame of mind for a reason. As the expression goes, "I had to go there!"

However, with this decision came a distraction when a woman's face appeared on my canvas. My Indian heritage seems to be taking the forefront. I remember my experience with sacred symbols (triangles, squares, circles, spirals, and crosses). Feeling that these shapes were keys to opening doorways to other dimensions, I seek the balance in potential.

I become overwhelmed, as I had been with the sand paintings. So many elements, so many levels, so many colors, so many shapes, and above all the pressure of time. The doorway often opened in a flash and could close just as quickly. Dare I open the door by picking up my brush? Would this adventure lead to positive results, or was I dumpster-diving, groping through garbage that should have been thrown away a long time ago.

CHAPTER 34

The Wheat Field

One tirelessly works in the fields getting ready for harvest.

Looking at the canvas I had started, I saw some creature looking back at me, but the canvas was chaotic and uninspired, as far as color. I saw a pyramid that needed a side, so I began there. I began extending the brush strokes across the canvas in horizontal strokes. Each stroke defined some direction and created some form. I was blindly stumbling in the dark trying to discover the form lurking, waiting for the light to identify it. If I recognized the form too early, I would lose it, trying to complete the form according to my perception, not the reality. I was preparing layers of paint and intent, creating an atmosphere of experience, until the rain, snow, fog, and sun exploded into a brilliant display of light and balance. I OPENED THE DOOR.

After hours of stroking the canvas, a vase of flowers turned into a wheat field. THE CAT MEOWS. I was trying to create a pathway through the wheat field to the sun shining at the top of the canvas. Just when I thought I had the path, it closed in on me. I had three horizontal bands of experience. Then in between one second and another, a door opened, and a flood of emotion hit me like a hailstorm on a sunny day. I gasped, and tears convulsed through the maelstrom. I kept painting, adding pure colors, red and blue and lavender. The atmosphere was changing once again. I identified circular movements and placed strokes to secure the shape. The three bands began to connect more closely and a vertical movement played through each of them. I felt a worker in the fields, lower right-hand corner. Van Gogh was here, working in the fields. I also noticed animal shapes in the fields, perhaps horses? – yes, horses. The power animal horse represents movement and power. I turned the canvas and recognized elephants and bird/animal creatures and a spiraling cypress tree. The color was still restrained, but some essence was materializing. The hour was late, and I had to find some way to get home. Easy enough if one is totally here in this earth reality, but I had been far away, and I was not back yet.

On the way home, I managed to stop at the red lights and go with the green. I found myself home in my chair shaking, ravenously hungry, stuffing my mouth and stomach with earth food, and trying to ground myself. I was in some sort of shock. "Just accept", I kept telling myself, but I had jet lag. I was irritable, and forces were pulling my attention to some other field. I raged at the toilet, which was running, and THE CAT WOULD NOT SHUT UP. My body felt heavy and sluggish as if my feet of clay were stuck in quicksand. I raged that earth reality always demanded so much from me. I had to keep struggling to buy and prepare food that nurtured me, and why couldn't the toilet work without my always having to check if it had stopped running? Simple earthly necessities drove me crazy. How could I concentrate on one world when another one took all my energy and focus? If I completely focused on my painting, I knew my earthly life would improve, but bouncing back and forth only made it difficult to reach the necessary depth or level to quiet my soul. And yet I also knew that my body could only take a limited time of this type of intense exploration. But my body also wanted release and resolution. TORN BETWEEN TWO WORLDS WAS NOT AN EASY FEAT. I laughed to myself – perhaps I was a control freak. Letting go was difficult; acceptance even harder. I shivered as I felt "Horse magic" shoot up my body. I was not alone. "Relax, you will be fine, and things will get better." Aho!

November 14,2000

Coming from the wheat field painting, I felt bloating, tightness, and hardness in my midsection. My body was stiff and disconnected. Was Van Gogh still a shadow working in the wheat field, striving to harvest, striving to pull in the bounty? My body was telling me I had gathered Van Gogh's sheaves of wheat to be sifted through, separating the parts to be used appropriately. The time of healing was at hand. Speaking of hands, she had sensed the texture of his hands during dreamtime the night before. I surrendered, because no strength was left. I prayed for my power animals to take me to the healing place as I slept.

The Wheat Field

The next day I simply existed, waiting for the work to be done. Watching TV, I suddenly felt that the prayers had been answered. I felt the searing red energy melt into the cool green of the forest. My gratitude and release brought the cleansing rain, tears of relief. One wave of healing had occurred, but there would be others. I worked on my body, centering and releasing with Tai Chi exercises. The tightness was leaving, and I was now feeling a "cockiness" of attitude, anger, impatience, and purposeful strength. Van Gogh seemed to be making me aware of "HIS attitude." The emotion was not defeatist but victorious. My hands were ready to work once again; they were not crippled by futility, exasperation, and loss of soul. MY RAGE WAS NOW PURE: MY LOVE UNTEMPERED. I was so grateful for the helping spirits that had made possible this transformation and this deliverance from pain and suffering. I felt as if I were at an award ceremony, thanking the people who made my winning possible, saying "You know who you are." Yes, and she knew who she was, too! Hallelujah!

> Message from The *- angels -*
> *We were there - you were not alone. We cradled you when you were spent, reviving you.*
> *When you remove so much of your spirit to wander outside of your body, the body is in a*
> *"frozen limbo." When you return, the body must be re-initiated into life.* (2013)

November 15, 2000

I was watching a show on TV about forgiveness. The previous day I had painted and was filled with a "cocky" attitude about who I was. But forgiveness? – every moment of my life was colored by Van Gogh's work and his decisions regarding his life. What was I to do now? What did a successful career in painting symbolize, a vindication for myself or others? What was my responsibility to myself now? I wanted to play, to explore, to enjoy life. I was finding delight in the magic of the Van Gogh strokes, and I was adding my own colors to the tapestry, creating a balance, a stillness, a playfulness. I was creating a strength and daring and confidence not felt before. However, I also felt at times doubtful of my ability. Where was the middle ground? HOW COULD I LET THE GENIUS IN WITHOUT BECOMING ANGRY AT THE WORLD FOR NOT RECOGNIZING IT? And what if they did – how would it change the way I viewed myself? WAS MY LESSON ABOUT BEING ABLE TO RECEIVE WITHOUT LOSING MY CENTER? So much of this experience was out of my control. I was touching the magic, but were the "spells" controlling me? Clarity collided with confusion at every turn. Great success challenged ego, and EGO CRUMBLED UNDER POWERFUL ARCHETYPAL ENERGIES. I was on a roller coaster ride, and I was throwing up (or cleansing). I wanted to lie in my sacred circle and rest in the arms of the mother, be fed chicken soup, and enveloped in love, protection, and assurance in what I was doing. I wanted my faith strengthened and my trust solidified. Eagle said I was on the correct flight pattern, but the landscape would change from time to time, that I was still moving, still flying, still in business. I would make the dips, plunges, and ascents as needed. "Remember, you're riding the wind – make it your friend – don't fight it. Relax; enjoy it. You've worked hard for the privilege – now soar!!!!!!"

Message from The ~ *Angels* ~
*You are fulfilling a soul purpose and mission, and the reverberations
extend into infinity. No other "recognition" is needed.* (2013)

November 19, 2000

I went back to the studio to review the canvas I had been working on, but I was shocked – it didn't have the "zing" of light I experienced in the previous canvas. The strokes were there, but it needed more light. Perhaps it was the borders. I painted one side yellow, and the yellow creeped onto the painting, starting again to weave the colors. I had to make the transition from Van Gogh to Mya. Suddenly there was his face, red beard and hair flaming, but his face was on the right side of the canvas, causing an imbalance. Suddenly I saw a vertical movement dividing the canvas and a half circle or oval at the top. It was Van Gogh standing behind his easel!!! Then I felt a cross implanted on the entire canvas. As I reinforced this cross with strokes, I felt a small oval at the top left of the vertical pole – it was a key! Gold, copper, silver. I saw a building on the left that needed a door. Gold was the key to the door. A huge sweeping circle at the bottom connecting the two sides made itself known imperatively. Silver was the halo of this global earth. Copper grounded the left side and unified swirling colors. Van Gogh's face was now totally obliterated. The white paint suddenly grabbed my fingers and swept across and up the canvas, traveling up the pole and spilling over on both sides. One strong stroke of red and blue floated over every imaginable color covered by a pale yellow green blanket. Spirit had hit my canvas like a lightning storm. In that flash, everything that was before was transformed in this electrifying light. The power destroyed and created in one breath. Van Gogh was gone, and I was here. The cross and the circle melted in the gold and silvery light of a copper earth. The black crows had given its space to white eagles. I closed the door to my studio and opened the door to my home. The cat needed to be fed.

Language always seemed to be inadequate in describing the painting process, but now the words were a comfort. THEY HELPED CLOSE THE DOOR.

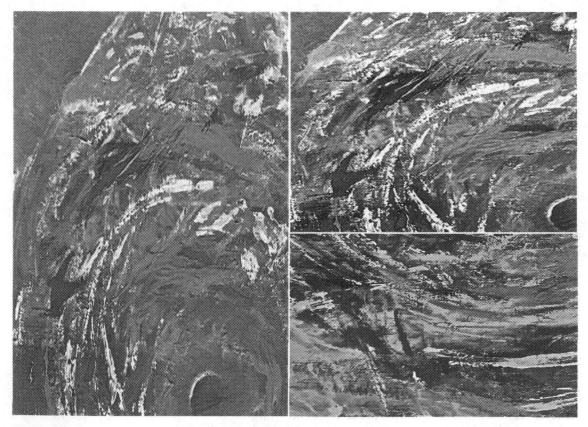

I AM HERE!

CHAPTER 35

Reincarnation

An artist reincarnates daily, dissolving old forms into new ones.

<u>THE INDIAN MAIDEN</u>
I remember your hands
Your strength
I remember your long braids
Your trail of tears
I remember your courage
Your resolve.
I remember your eyes of brown
Your flecks of green
I remember your skin of gold
Your copper skins
I remember your silver beads
Your turquoise circles
I remember your love
Your tenderness
I remember your journey
Your defeats and victories
I remember when you said
Take your heart and embrace
The rays of gold
Take your heart and forget
The arrows
Take your heart and see
The blue of healing

Take your heart and soar
Over the ocean.

November 24, 2000

Strange that as soon as Van Gogh was transformed, memories of an Indian life permeated my consciousness. The two lives were connected in some inexplicable way. The story was not complete; another chapter was unfolding. Kyalaka from the Land of Dreams whispered in her ear, "Remember, remember."

I visioned how Van Gogh would respond to the Southwest and the Native Americans, and somehow I sensed he was simpatico with honoring the Earth as The Mother - living in harmony with the land - experiencing Spirit in all things - going on Vision Quest for a new dream. I felt Spirit rushing through my body, confirming that I was on the right path.

In this life about 10 years ago, I experienced being called to this part of the country – the Southwest – canyons, blue skies, pueblos, and white smoke. When I arrived, in a vision I was greeted by the Indian people, who brought me gifts as if I were to fulfill some prophecy. I had no idea what that was, but I had abandoned my other existence to make the journey – to be on the land. Somehow the land would help me recall what I had come to do.

JOURNAL:

My parents never understood why I had to complete the mission or answer the call when they were here on earth; but from the other side, I suspect they have come to understand. My sons may not understand the details, but I feel they would support me and would want me to follow my dream. Something in what I was about to do would bring peace to their hearts as well as to my own. I recalled the Indian Spirit names I had given my two boys in a healing ceremony. My sons' names were written in the Book of Dreams. In that place, all dreams were embraced – spirit and soul soared together – unconditional love and acceptance opened every door – peace and power laid down together like the lion and lamb. I did not put their names there to follow any rules or to "save them." I put their names there out of love and respect for their free will, their freedom, and a trust in Spirit's plan for them.

love them so much that my heart seems to expand at just the thought of them, but I didn't need them to be bound to my individual dream. They are free to dream their own dreams, and I will fight for their right to do so.

As I was writing, The Red Shawl flashed in my mind's eye; the dancing shawl I had purchased at the Pow Wow with four beautiful embroidered eagles holding the four directions. As the red shawl was gently placed in my hands, I promised its maker that I would dance with it and paint its power – the power of the eagle's flight. I cradled my new purchase and walked out into the dream.

The red shawl represented the blood shed for my dream… my life force… my spirit energy. It was my wings of flight, my eyes of vision, my warrior's heart. I would dance in my circle and remember.

I AM

The Angel of the Indigenous Peoples

I honor your visions and your willingness to listen to Spirit. I hold you in the
Sacred Wheel in the Sky where you commune with your Power Animals and
Your Guides. I affirm your innate understanding of Mother Earth and Father
Sky, and I bless you with the gifts of both. I have always been with you on the
Good Red Road, and I welcome you when you leave your earthly existence.

My mind was being pulled back again to Michelangelo – to the secrets of his work and what those secrets had to do with me now. As always when I had questions "too big" to comprehend, I consulted Kyalaka. Her answer follows:

"You and he are connected by a bloodline of warriors. He was instantly transformed by his paintings. He remembered the fall from grace. He remembered the beauty of the soul. He remembered how small his life was in relation to the dream. He stood alone against the most powerful forces. He knew others would not see what he had painted in his masterpiece, "The Last Judgment" – he knew they would transpose their own dreams on his creation, but there was still something in those paintings that could not be reinterpreted or changed – his spirit. And Mary appears twice. The love is in the Mother.

Michelangelo understood on one level the tremendous task he had been given, but through Spirit he performed and executed a vision not to imagined in any place other than the Land of Dreams. He displayed superhuman strength, courage, determination, and love while in the dream. When he returned, time caught up to his earthly body and age melted his faculties, but oh, he had seen the other side, and he would go home again. Beauty would paint him, and love would sculpt his form into the next creation – the next lifetime.

December 4, 2000

JOURNAL:

Here I am. The "I" is a mystery. The more I know about myself the more I realize there is so much more to know. I do know I want to celebrate life – not just its joys but also its sorrows and frustrations. I laugh as I struggle with my aches and pains and my body's groans and "ahhs." I laugh as I solve momentous problems, only to find the problems changing face and appearing on stages as other characters in a plot that demands new stage settings. I laugh as I deliberate each morning where I'm going, what I will do, and when I will do it (as if it mattered). I laugh as I contemplate what foods I will give my body, and I realize even that transforms and has to be excreted, questioning a system whereby there has to be waste at all. I laugh as I try things I hate, finding out that I love them, and try things I love, and find I hate them. I laugh as I contemplate what I want and realize it is a fantasy, a myth of misperception. I laugh as I make goals, trying to be responsible for what I create only discovering that creation itself is the goal and that destruction is its facilitator. I laugh as I spin around and around in my creations, in my world of mind.

I laugh as I cling to illusion and reject reality. I laugh as I feel trapped in a moment, afraid to take in the breath of the next moment. I laugh as I meet people with cold and hooded eyes and stumble into other eyes reflecting universes, boundless understanding, and knowingness. I laugh and laugh as I posture, gesture, and articulate. I laugh at my journeys to the studio to spend time stripping my masks only to find others underneath. I laugh at my attempt to know who "I" am.

WE LIVE IN A HALL OF MIRRORS, WHERE THE CRACKED MIRROR IS THE FIRST SIGN THAT THE REFLECTION IS A PROJECTED ILLUSION. We are not the image – the crack or wound is the entry into wholeness – into reality – into the dream from which we came.

December 24, 2000

JOURNAL:

I seem to be painting for seven generations, bringing each canvas to some conclusion, or balance. Each stroke was a moment in time, each color its vibration, and each tone between the white and black keys of a musical scale. Impulses for spirals, serpentine squiggles, dots and dashes, and cross-hatching strokes flowed from my fingers. Fields of wild growth under blazing suns, paths through undergrowth, haystacks, windmills, fig trees, and flowering fields. Yellow and lilac, orange and blue, red and green. Gold, bronze, copper, and silver. The black crows were always there in the distance waiting. The laborer in the fields or Van Gogh, the Sower, walking through creation was always there. Movement was always there. The still point was always there. I worked bringing the crescendo to a peak, obliterating caution and control… the crescendo destroying or intensely bringing all that came before into a moment where nothing else existed.

I asked Spirit to let me see through the eyes of the child, eyes innocent with glory, eyes curious with no fear, and eyes full of love and wonder. I found circles that began expanding out into the whole. I found nothing could be contained. Everything was a part of every other thing. Colors danced, and light played, but I was in the SPACE BETWEEN THE DOOR OPENING AND

THE DOOR CLOSING. When the door opened, there were no limits; when the door closed, boundaries were set. I was flying into unknown dimensions, causing me to be unable to find the door to Earth. Even when I closed the door to a certain painting, I suffered jet lag, body aches, and exhaustion. I questioned whether I could survive this needing to know… Was it a mistake or an imbalance?… Would my body survive the search?… would my mind be able to heal or contain the energy?… was I substituting painting for living a "real life?" Was I rejecting reality for a fantasy or rejecting a fantasy for a reality? Could I do both, and was each supporting the other? After all, wasn't caution and tentativeness an ineffective or impotent decision in painting OR in life?

If we are here, then we must be bold or we spit on our uniqueness and our perfect wholeness and the pain and suffering it took to get here. MANY LIVES may be necessary to "touch the dream" or touch "the awakening." I felt the spirits of so many artists in my heart - countless warriors paving the way. Their strife, pain, and suffering were my own, but what was also my own was the presence of strength and courage in the midst of unbelievable challenges and odds. I sensed their voices, their determination, their spirits soaring. If time and space are illusionary, their voices are in the here and now for those who can hear. Listen to the sound of imagination breaking through the dullness, when love points to wholeness, when Jesus's example points to our own divinity, when our own uniqueness points to our higher calling, when veils of illusion give way to the light of truth.

I AM

The Angel of Time.

I bring all your lifetimes together in one dream of exquisite Beauty. I remind you that you are much more than you ever imagined. Your lives have been an offering to reveal the truth beyond time and space. You are the epitome of greatness and splendor!

Your crystal wings have carried you far!

CHAPTER 36

Love

The question is: In spite of everything, can you still love?

DECEMBER 27, 2000

Love is the basis or the root of all things – even if that which is created is despair. Longing for the love of the universal Mother or soulmate suggests some fractal in our DNA, some buried memory, or some forgotten wholeness. To create anything depends on a love for something – man, woman, child, self, object, idea, concept, vision, dream. Perhaps our journey will become easier as our bodies become more accustomed to the vibration of love. In the meantime, our bodies may reflect a conflict, or we may see discrepancies between the inner and outer worlds of experience. This discrepancy can cause our bodies to be strained under the influence of this discordance. I certainly feel my body talk of these things in pain and disorientation.

Love is the glue by which we stick our experiences together. Love shows us the connections between these seemingly random experiences much like paper-doll cutouts joined at the fold. To remove any cutout would break the accordion chain of events, which would in turn reek havoc on the cohesiveness of spirit. Perhaps that's why scientists have been working on decoding DNA for so long because the source of love is intangible in the DNA strand.

Love helps us bear our density of earthly life and prevents us from going back to spirit too soon. I AM CONVINCED THE LOVE I FEEL FOR MY SONS AND THE LOVE THEY FEEL FOR ME HAS SAVED MY LIFE MANY TIMES OVER.

One such experience took place in a hospital where I had been for months with pneumonia and a high fever. I began seeing resignation and defeatism and long faces around me, and the Church sent someone "to save me" or to remind me of my sins and to warn me to do what they said in order for me to enter the Kingdom of God. This "someone" did not offer love but judgment and anger that I had not "woke up" to their truth. In a way they did "save me," not in the way they intended but by giving me anger to fight back. I had a 6 month old son, and I did NOT intend to leave him.

Love always finds its mark. Poets and philosophers for centuries have led "monk-like" existences, pouring their love in poems and letters. The question is not "Do you have someone to love you, but CAN you love – no matter what? Anger, violence, and destruction are part of creation in the sense that they are still in relationship to love or the lack of love. If you destroy all those things within that are not in love – "what is left is Love." If we project our lovelessness, we try to destroy the object on which we have projected. Women throughout the ages have been the recipients of such projections. The witch hunts, the genital mutilation of women and girls, the domination and slavery of women, the killing of girl babies, the economical inequality in the workforce, the racial prejudice, and Holy War after Holy War. IF WE LOOK WITHIN OURSELVES AND LOVE ALL THOSE PLACE - THE SHADOW AND THE LIGHT - WE WILL SEE WITH NEW EYES AND A NEW HEART.

Driving down the mountain in 1998, I had to slow down for a couple of dogs who had gotten away from their owner. Cars were pulled over trying to assist the owner in retrieving her dogs. For some reason, the scene tugged at some distant memory. Suddenly the question formed in my mind, "Have I ever been truly loved?" I thought of the love of my sons, and that love was powerful beyond belief, but in this moment, my heart went to another love. *"Yes. Theo loved me."*

My body relaxed as I remembered, and the remembered love eased my anguish and urgency.

I sensed other loves throughout the ages, ones displaying all the colors of the rainbow and then others up the spectrum into the ethers. There were loves twin in nature, each one connected to the other, almost as one. The healing love of a woman was there which can literally extend life. A "believing" love was also there - a love that supports the other and holds the space for possibilities.

I needed a "believing mirror." I didn't want to be viewed solely as a product or as one who had achieved some successful technique or methodology. I wanted outside validation of the importance of art in our world and in our minds.

I was thinking of art, not in the usual sense… the art as a business or the art as a hobby of sorts or even the art that is used as propaganda for some advancing ideology. Perhaps I was thinking of art in its purity, its inability to be corrupted or misaligned or controlled. I wanted the support for such an art to be valued by communities, countries, the world, and to see the tremendous benefits and bounty embraced.

In a conference call on May 23, 2013:

I asked Neale Donald Walsch, "How can we educate people to the fact that art can change the world?" In his answer, he explained that when we help people to understand the function of art, they will once again support art. "It's storytelling - humanity telling stories to themselves about themselves."... that's why we support the arts - not because it creates a cultural PERSON, no, but art creates an entire society and what that society thinks about itself.

Look at what our television is doing to us - look at what video games are doing to us. Look at what ignoring the arts has done to us - WAKE UP!"

He says, "the purpose of all art is to return us to ourselves."[18]

David Paladin, visionary artist, says that many of the storytellers were also shamans...."The shaman creates a story that is plausible and acceptable for the moment, always recognizing that the stories change with time as truth continues to grow and evolve. Absolute beliefs prevent us from responding creatively. Our beliefs should never be so absolute that we can't move beyond them, recreate them, or see them from another perspective."...[19]

If love is the glue by which we stick our experiences together, then art becomes the universal language connecting what gives meaning, power, and heart to our lives.

---

18 www.humanitiesteam.org.

19 *PAINTING THE DREAM (THE VISIONARY ART OF NAVAJO PAINTER DAVID CHETHLAHE PALADIN)* by DAVID CHETHLAHE PALADIN, p. 25.

CHAPTER 37

Accepting the Challenge

**If we have the capacity to create the illusion, we have the
capacity to create and know the reality.**

When Mya looked at what it would mean to be "handed the torch" from Van Gogh and others, she agreed with the artist Gauguin that whatever knowledge each artist acquired from within and kept pure from outside influences could be handed down to other artists, and this knowledge could become great.

How would she respond to any knowledge passed on to her? She considered several options. Would she carry on the pursuit of art in the plastic sense, or would she live a life that was artful (or both)? Did it mean "fame" or "anonymity?" Which would be more powerful? Would she concentrate on learning the tools of the trade and creating "products" that would then be accessible for display and sale, or would she live basically a "hermit's life," making her discoveries and experiencing their revelations in the cloister of her own individual mind/soul/body.

Although she was extremely motivated and captivated by her concrete creations, she saw them next to the context in which they were created – "her story." How could one painting or a thousand paintings tell that story? The creations were plastic paint on a two dimensional frame hanging in space. She saw them as living and moving dramas, but could others see them in that LIGHT? They were entities that moved and breathed anonymously. How could she market (or should she) such intangible forces? How could she sell her ANGELS? Was the "story" bigger than the individual expression?

In a way, yes, because the story embraced every other individual expression, but the story was in the paint for those who could read it. Mya realized she was contradicting herself when she railed against the public ignoring the work for a "desirable" story, but she also realized that what she experienced when she painted was as important or more expansive than the actual painting. The story told the world– "You, too, can use art to define, refine, and transform your life. Not only can you use art in the plastic sense, you can use the broader meaning of art to touch and mold every 'object' and 'subject' of your existence. YOU WILL NEVER EVER BE A VICTIM AGAIN!!!! Van Gogh's color swirls, Michelangelo's stone sentinels, and my soul memories SCREAM through the illusion of limitation.

But not all eyes can see, and not all hearts are open. Mya remembered an incident that so exemplified this fact. Her painting had been chosen for an exhibit downtown, and she was excited to be part of a gathering, viewing art. She looked around and didn't see anyone on her list of invitations; so, she was feeling a bit abandoned and in alien territory.

There was the usual intellectual conversation about the ideas and concepts around the work with artists explaining or relating their credentials and successes to the prospective buyers. Mya wandered about, trying to feel comfortable in this environment while actually feeling like a fish out of water. She was in her environment of art but not a part of this scene. She ended up talking more to the bartender than anyone else; he seemed the most friendly and open. Of course, that was what he was paid for.

Then she noticed another fish out of water in the gallery. He did not have the "dress" that was appropriate for a gallery opening; in fact, he was dirty and slovenly dressed. However, as she was standing in front of her painting, this out-of-place man came and stood beside her. He asked, "Is this your painting?" I said, "Yes!" The painting had three figures in it, one being an angel. He began describing my painting to me as if he could see underneath the plastic paint to the thoughts and feelings I had before picking up the brush. She was shocked beyond belief!!!! How did he know? How could he see so accurately? And where did he come from, this homeless vagabond off the streets?

Others in the gallery were concerned about this man and the fact that Mya was talking to him at great length. Many felt the need to warn her; this was not a man to be trusted. They thought he wanted something from Mya, some money or a meal, etc. He was judged to be dangerous. Even the guard on duty for the evening was keeping an eye on him.

—

She writes: And yet in the whole of the evening, I did not hear any words so true, poignant, and powerful as the words from this homeless man - this supposedly unscripted surprise encounter. I knew that what he said came from another source or that because of his circumstances, his heart was open and his vision unimpaired by pomp and circumstance.

At some point outside, with the guard looking on, he revealed to me that he was alienated from his daughter and wanted to call her. I encouraged him to call his daughter and make amends. Some might say that this was an attempt on his part for sympathy or a means to lure me into some other scenario. But what if the true intents were not important and what was important was the underlying SACRED TRUTH of what was accomplished that night… the healing of emotions and the exercise of empathy and compassion. Two people, feeling lost, happened upon one another in one minute span of time and was able to give each other a gift of understanding and empathy.

And what of the other people at that gallery that night. I did not know - perhaps they were connecting to other points on the spectrum. I, however, was not drawn to participate any further; there seemed to be no warmth or authentic expression. Perhaps I was in the midst of the earth's collective dream.

I AM

The Angel that brings HEALING.

I take many forms, but I use color and light to bring wholeness and unity. I heal broken dreams, broken hearts, and broken wings. I use all the colors of the rainbow to reflect the purity of the WHITE LIGHT, but GREEN HEALS the HEART and BLUE HEALS the FEAR that limits its expression.

I AM the Angel of Healing

Although the collective dream was always present, I was interested in how the individual dream was connected to the divine dream and how it could evolve and transform earth reality. I was convinced that fulfillment and prosperity were possible when the two dreams were twinned or in synch.

Mya's higher self seemed to take over and give her this message:

The divine dream is not a conditioning or a manipulation; it is your truth, undiluted by the chemicals of fear, false guilt, and shame. Death is but an opportunity to chase your rainbow, to ride the wings of the eagle, to remember a higher love. This death produces a life of gold after the alchemical fire. What we fear is change — change of how we see ourselves to be and attachment to same. Our lives are what we have created in conjunction to how much freedom we can embrace. Our lives are the extent of our capacity to love all things (even the illusion.) If we have the capacity to create the illusion, we have the capacity to create and know the reality.

Go as into "rehab." Find out how the drug of fear is controlling you. There is a "you" underneath the mask that is a multidimensional being with many faces, but all a part of "you."

You are what you think — the universe will respond to your responsibility of thought. The universe will reveal the solidity of your new vision of yourself. This book is written as one person's individual dream... one person's thoughts, wishes, and reflections. For others, do you recognize stirrings of your own soul and spirit? Do you remember dreams and other lifetimes buried within your own consciousness? The story is a split second in time. Like the splitting of the atom, other worlds are created by that one action.

You have only one challenge. Will you be responsible for what you dream?

Use your higher mind to perceive what is possible. Co-create with the divine to continue the dream - the evolution of yourself and the God/Goddess within.

YOU ARE THE FORM — you are the vehicle — you are the clay pot. Hold your humanness and your divinity within that clay pot that is of the earth and watch your dreams (children) be born and multiply. Your immortality depends on picking up the torch *and handing it on to the next runner. Listen for the voices on the wind — perhaps you will hear your own twin flame, soulmate, past life, or helping spirit whisper in your ear —* DREAM!

December 30, 2000

I sensed that Van Gogh realized his work was beyond the physical, the mental, and the emotional or whatever suggested illness or malady affected his brain. He may not have understood the story, but he was determined to respond as long as he could. Whatever happened that day he died was not a "giving up" or "giving in," and I truly believe that centuries of historians have asked the wrong questions about Van Gogh's life.

My life has extended the story within the story, and my work with art, as a healing agent, hopefully has touched many lives and other stories within the garment of reality.

In the past, while searching for my place in society, I felt compelled to bring art to those who seemed to need healing -convicts, confused teens, children, abused women, the addicted, the saints and sinners, schizophrenics, manic-depressives, and those with developmental disabilities. I worked as a volunteer in these arenas, wanting to give these souls a tool for healing, a tool of empowerment, a tool for feeling their spirits. Sometimes, in turn, they taught me something about "spirit" and "inner knowing." But through it all, the "expression" of a human and their soulfulness was a beautiful thing to witness.

CHAPTER 38

The Colors

Colors cascading like a waterfall, telling me who I am.

JANUARY 7, 2001

Mya writes: That accursed hat! I have a straw hat that I bought for the beach. I have found a place for this hat on the wall of every house. I have no idea why or what that hat means to me, but it's presence on the wall makes me feel that no one but me could live here. The hat was a sign I was home!

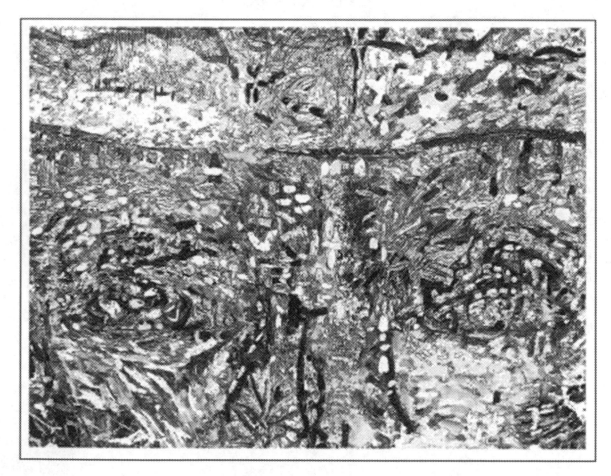

Man With the Hat

I was feeling the need to expand my vision – paint on larger surfaces. I felt my fingers tingling with urgency. I could not afford artist's paints because of the amount of paint I was heaping on the canvasses, so I followed a lead about a line of house paints that were metallic in nature. I was obsessed with the properties of these paints and their relationship to the light. I gathered my courage and went shopping for paint. What I found astounded me. Van Gogh's prophecy of new paints echoed in my ears. He believed that the inquiry into the nature of color would be taken up by a future generation and continued thereafter. He also hinted at different chemical properties of paints.[20]

Now I was seeing charts and charts of every imaginable SHADE. I wanted them all. I had to have them ALL. But what of money? I wrestled and wrestled with the thought of the cost and investment, and deep inside me, an anger arose. Why shouldn't I have my colors? Why should my hands be tied, my throat constricted by this lack of means to express what I needed to express? At the same time, I wondered why the colors were so important to me.

Then she remembers.... remembers the day the colors went away. She was five years old, sitting under a tree in a barren Oklahoma landscape. She was sifting sand with a screen, watching the grains of sand, according to gravity, form layers of hills and valleys.

"I felt the sand sift until each grain was the same combining with other grains to form structures of such magnificent beauty. I was mesmerized by the light hitting these forms creating shadows and highlights. I felt safe. As the light hit the crystals of sand, rainbow colors spiraled out into the air. Soon these spirals began to dance with one another in joyous ecstasy. I felt completely safe and part of a reality that was "real" and harmonious. The colors were not objects or visions, but essences – the presence of friends, of playmates, of loving and accepting family. I felt so loved and accepted and treasured. At the time, I did not question who or what the colors were – I just played. Hours and hours passed in this DREAMLAND OF REALITY.

Spending time here made everything else bearable. But one day I realized that some of the colors were leaving, and I could not get them back. I cried and cried. I think maybe I sent them away because I stopped believing in them. Those around me did not believe in the colors and thought I was wasting my time. I kept hearing, "It's JUST your imagination." The non-support made me question my experience and question the safety of my environment. I became afraid, and I didn't feel safe anymore. As I began to live in fear, the colors could not breathe anymore. I did not know what to do – so I told the colors to wait for me in a safe place, and I would come and get them one day. (tears)

---

20 Vol. III, page 231.

As the days went by, shades of yellow, red, blue, purple, green began to sift out of my consciousness. "You must try to be good, but you will never be" saw shades of marvelous clay colors drift away. "You must not say what you think" took lavender blues out into the mist. "You must obey" took creamy mauves out like a light. "Girls are not as good as boys" took orangish tinges of pink and white. Competition and jealousy took 9,000 shades of green and yellow. There was one day, in particular, I shall never forget. My sense of self and safety was forever changed. That day I lost almost all of the reds, and I ceased to exist as I had before. I had lost the colors, and now I was but a shadow. I wasn't sure how others could see me, as I no longer was there. I was in the safe place with all the colors. My physical reality was the color of sand without the rainbow colors. The only thing that kept me from totally disappearing was the owl. The owl seemed to visit me regardless whether I believed it was real. The owl told me the truth even when my life was a lie. The owl gave me hope that one day I would be able to trust myself again. THE OWL WAS ALWAYS THERE. Later, I came to realize the owl was a "power animal" that had come to protect and guide me. a manifestation of truth that was hidden.

I was to live that lie for 55 years, until my body began to reflect the death I felt in my soul. Over a span of 25 years, I began painting, retrieving some of the colors. But as I did, I experienced the pain of that day when I let the colors go. I knew I had to bring them back – but no one told me how. NO ONE EVEN ACKNOWLEDGED THAT THE COLORS WERE PIECES OF MY SOULD THAT COULD NOT LIVE WITH THE LIE. No one held me as I sobbed, racked by the grief of knowing such splendor and losing it. No one acknowledged my pain or encouraged me, attaching negative concepts to my behavior - I suppose hoping to shake me out of my "supposed delusion." But the owl knew the truth, and some part of me did, too.

CHAPTER 39

The Handprint

The warm and fuzzy software of the cold computer age...

FEBRUARY 7, 2001

~

I had resisted computer technology with both hands and feet. I felt that my art was becoming extinct – the actual "real-time" of my creations – the virtual layering of time and experience – the texturing of a moment's impulse – the color of dimensions visited – the light of love. I was frustrated with taking photos of my work - the photo was another creation apart from the original work. That creation was designed through a camera lens – flattened and compressed. Added to these differences was the light of the sun and the surrounding area. I could take those photos and put them into the computer, changing the color, tint, shape, and texture; in fact, I could change almost everything about those photos, producing countless additional creations. But the photo was not real – the files in my computer were not real. WAS I LOSING SOMETHING OF THE ORIGINAL HANDPRINT IMPORTANT FOR THE SPECIES AS A WHOLE?

I write: Losing the handprint is losing the dream – a dream that can't be replaced or re-dreamed. So where was I? The new technology was not going away. How could I use it and still retain my integrity? Where was the heartbeat in all this?

I was always dissatisfied with the finished product because it didn't tell the story of how it had been born. I didn't like works of art that were sold on story alone or works based on competition, fame, and fortune. How could the story and the art merge to tell the truth?

I had read many accounts of how language could not adequately describe art since the tools of art were a language in itself and so totally subjective. O.K. So I have technology, art, language, and subjectivity. How can I impart the power of the work when I have to rely on the viewer's capacity to see and feel with the heart. How can I tell the story in paint when light, environment, and technology distort the original "happening?" I WANTED TO IMPART WITH THE PIECE OF ART AN AWARENESS OF THE EXPERIENCE FROM WHICH IT CAME.

In one fatal sweep of inspiration, I saw the way. If computers could produce virtual reality for video games, education, and global knowledge, why couldn't it produce virtual reality for the painting of a painting? I projected into the future bringing the past and present with me. Computers were based on the crystal – conduction and transmitting electrical impulses. Large frame computers had been reduced from the size of a large room to the size of a laptop and even smaller.

As the years passed through my consciousness, I saw reduction after reduction until the mechanism was a small as a pebble held in the palm of the hand. Technology had figured a way to combine the individual soul or spirit with the tools to receive unaffected, uninfluenced information. This information was "programmed" according to the imprint or blueprint of the individual. Part of this technology was reinforced by discoveries over the years regarding DNA or the genome. New uses and properties of the crystal were discovered, and color, or rays of light, were discovered to be encoded messages. These messages were shared by all through the artist or the visionary.

The truth was that this information has been shared for eons of time subconsciously because our thoughts change reality. However, technology found a way to make this information conscious and perceptible as never before. Machines had been devised to make the experience "real" to all. The artist was "hooked up" to machines that in turn translated his experience, not only in color, but also in time, heartbeat, breath, and emotion.

I flashed to my projection of my experience with Michelangelo when I had picked up the pebble, which had transported me and Michelangelo in time. The machines, wires, and electrical impulses had been reduced to a small pebble held in the hand.

It was time to experience.

2005 – The room was darkened. The "screen" occupied the whole room, ceiling, floor, and walls. The subject was one of my paintings. The viewer enters and sits inside a circular space. All around him are small pebbles of light and a pair of glasses coated in white-gold. The viewer puts the glasses on and contemplates which stone to pick up and embrace. The pink one invites. So – the pink one it is. What would the experience be? As soon as the stone cradled the palm – a heartbeat was heard, and a kind of rising and falling of breath. A blank white screen appears. A stroke appears with an inhalation – a pause as the heart races. Slow tentative strokes follow more pauses as the dance begins. Then a mushing of three colors pushing, pulling, lightly touching. Then as more colors and strokes are added, the heartbeat seems to suspend its beating into a frozen space where time stands still, but the strokes move so rapidly as to not be perceived. The strokes are flying at such a rate as to separate from the artist and viewer, separate from thought, from caution, from intent. These "sessions" continue until the last stroke is applied. The painting is complete. The totality produces a heart response of the artist and the viewer. What was seen with the eyes was also felt with the heart.

I pulled out of the dream. I knew now why I had to leave a marriage of 30 years. I had to incubate and find a friendly and supportive environment to dream this dream and many others. I needed a dark embryonic fluid in which to dream. The marriage was dominated by my husband's dream, and I had to claim my own dream. Suddenly I realized I had given him a gift by leaving – an allowance, a freedom – to dream his dream without contamination. I had given the same gift to myself.

At the time I didn't know what was in store or what would be created in this new space; I was stepping out blindly as MY OWN ADVOCATE! I must love myself enough to not "settle" and to give myself the chance to love GRANDER - to hold the space for that possibility, that probability, that potential.

I had gone over the scenario countless times seeking the "right" decision, the "logical, spiritual, and emphatic" reason to walk away from the marriage. Now peace washed over me like a warm ocean wave, and I knew that my action was appropriate and timely.

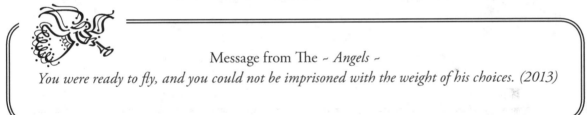

Message from The - *Angels* -
You were ready to fly, and you could not be imprisoned with the weight of his choices. (2013)

When a soul life is threatened, dreams are born. The psyche fights for itself to express - NOT TO BE HELD DOWN. These parts of ourselves deserve attention and love, and no army or lesser dream can stand in its way.

I came out of my reverie about the divorce to vision once again, projecting on other ways the viewer could "experience" a work of art. The "realtime" of each stroke was important, but also what went on before and after that work of art… what was in front of and behind the canvas. Information must be measured about what aspect of the dream was triggered and how the "alive" work continued. My mind was exploding into crystals of light. Certainly intent would be a trigger point, but what was the intent of the completed work? What door would open to this new child of creation?

Van Gogh died in 1890 and now in 2014 a website on the internet and facebook presented a title that caught my eye --- Van Gogh - Alive Exhibition - an unforgettable multi-sensory exhibition traveling around the world. What could be more "virtual" than columns of flashing pictures, paintings, and writings corresponding to a harmonic symphony of music.

I remembered again that in the Dune Series a painting by Van Gogh was held as a treasure. The technology of the future was used to capture a flourishing of information as to Van Gogh's feeling and genius to be relayed by simply touching the black dot on the corner of the frame.[21]

Part of the story of the painting was my steps going into the studio, the sights and smells of my journey to and from the studio. Nothing was immaterial. Currents of electricity were going everywhere, even invading my night dreams during the painting sessions. The shapes and symbols inside the paintings were also possibly being picked up by sensors from unknown locations. Did they communicate just as a series of dots and dashes or computer language of one's and zeros?

Just as a physical representation of a dog creates images and meanings, COULD NOT A CIRCLE OF A PARTICULAR COLOR TRANSLATE MEANING TO SOME UNKNOWN CULTURE? And what of the effect, response, or change? Would I receive the response from where ever in some bizarre and magical way? PAINTING WAS, AFTER ALL, A MEANS OF COMMUNICATION. I wondered if the messages were directed to some galaxy or some star, and what the effect would be.

Message from *- Archangel Michael -*
The golden light of the divine flows through your designs out into
the universes and multi-universes and all existence.

My teacher in Shamanism remarked once that when one goes to another dimension, all one sees is geometric shapes and colors until the forms can be translated. At the time I was painting simple, colored geometric designs with very little brushwork or variance within the colors. Surprisingly enough, this style came at a time when I felt I had crossed over some boundary that would enable me to be MORE expressive. Instead here were simple paint by number outlined forms as if in a coloring book. But what had come before was a painting in which I had connected with emotion as never before. IN THE NEW DESIGN I WAN'T SURE IF I WAS RETREATING FROM THE EMOTION, OR I HAD SIMPLY EMPTIED OUT ALL EMOTION. The geometric designs were joyful and untaxed and playful – like a child's free exploration… with no impending danger or rush in time.

After a few of these delights, another urge took over, and that was to paint with sand. My child was definitely at work creating her playground. I remembered again my experience sifting sand under the mesquite tree when I was 5 years old. Was there something healing about the sand itself? The Native Americans, the Tibetans, and other cultures certainly thought so.

---

21 *Chapterhouse: Dune* by Frank Herbert.

Kyalaka interjected: *Sand crystals are time in motion. They were once rocks, mountains, and ocean valleys. They reflect the light, and they shift with time.*

Did they hold complete cultures in their grainy substance? Did they have secrets to tell?

My sand paintings were created with these thoughts in mind in an attempt to bring spirits to rest and to heal. The layers of sand and glue shifted and formed small mountains and valleys – a terrain like some satellite view of a distant planet. I used some of the sand paintings to overlap old paintings, thus playing more with time.

Again I felt the importance of giving these paintings life – but I didn't have a clue in words as to their "real" life or innate qualities.

I was afraid of losing myself or falling into the past when I painted – wanting not to live in the past, but in the present. This resistance and acceptance shifted back and forth like the sand letting go of the heavier grains and rearranging the lighter ones - all this while dealing with the physicality of maintaining a body and a "life" on this plane. Writing cushioned the blows of my realizations. If I had carried all those thoughts in my brain – I would have short-circuited. SO ON THE WINGS OF WORDS - I SLOWLY SANK INTO THE WATER OF MY NEW DREAM. Still I was ill-prepared for the power of these new strokes. I spent many a day recuperating from the shock of what I had uncovered.

The integration of the layered sand crystals, the geometric design, and the emotional strokes came on the scene like a typhoon blowing and howling until the weather changed once again. Words flew in again to prepare the nervous system for the next phase… to make connections and to link distant thoughts in relation to the swirling paint and colors.

The sandwich looked like this – the bottom piece of bread was the emotional painting before the geometric designs. It released emotion… not only released emotion in front of the canvas but actually put the loneliness IN THE PAINT. Next came the formation of a new world in the raw stuff of life – circles, triangles, squares, etc. (the meat of the sandwich). Next came the lettuce and tomatoes – the sand paintings – the added flavor, complementing and balancing. Lastly came the top slice of bread – the return to passion, but with a structured base.

THE SHAPES ARE THE VESSELS ON THE SEA OF EMOTIONS,
PREPARING TO REACH A NEW LAND, A NEW SHORE.

Van Gogh's Redemption

CHAPTER 40

Fractals
(love and light)

DECEMBER 2001

⌒

I was thinking of fractals and how they related to love, God, and art. I decided to ask Kyalaka. Kyalaka said:

Fractals are what the name implies, a fragment of a whole. Within every living thing, including rocks and trees, are fractals. Colors and shapes and light that describe a consciousness. A human being is a fractal. Under closer inspection, every particle of light has within it a code as to its source. Within every value of color is a story relating to its environment. Fractals are infinite. The DNA can be read as a fractal. A body part down to a hair, or a fingerprint or a nail can be read as a fractal. A PAINTING CAN BE READ AS A FRACTAL.

Love answers all questions. What you love sends energy back to you in appreciation. What you hate denies your very existence and sends back the energy of rejection. Love refracts the energy into other organisms. Hate is a black hole. It is not devoid of light, but it is a light that absorbs itself and does not reflect or refract. WHEN YOU ACCEPT YOUR HATE AS YOUR OWN DARKNESS, YOU CAN ACTUALLY LOVE IT AND BRING IT LIGHT.

Color is the spectrum of light. There are infinite black holes waiting for the light – and color is the pathway – the locator of a particular environment or black hole. White is not pure in the sense you think of it; it is all the black holes receiving light.

Light is that essence of love we seek but cannot seem to grasp because we are fractals of a whole – a one. We are all a color on the spectrum, not only a color but a value or tint of a color – combining the light and dark of us. No one color or tint is supreme. They all combine to create a symphony of unbelievable beauty and harmony. Your one dominant tint, or melody, encompasses other rhythms and beats. IT PRODUCES THE SONG YOU ALONE CAN SING IN THE CHOIR OF HEAVEN!

The subtle underlying rhythms of the song are as important as the main melody because it sets the stage or possibility for the song to be heard. WHAT IS DARK OR UNCLEAR AFFECTS THE DREAM AND DRAWS TO IT THAT WHICH WILL GIVE IT LIGHT. Everything gets what it needs with no error or mistaken adjustment. All songs are fractals pointing to yet another range of sound. There are no accidents, only a SUPREME LOVING PRESENCE THAT IS THE CONDUCTOR. There is no tragedy or injustice. YOU ARE IN A DREAM IN WHICH YOU DRAW TO YOU WHAT YOU NEED TO AWAKEN FROM THE DREAM - TO AWAKEN SO THAT YOUR SOUL CAN REMEMBER.

Other lifetimes are fractals that are reflected in your present. They all can change in the dream you are dreaming now. Everything is based on the lucidity of your dream. Are you going to choose what happens, or are you going to allow the dream to dream you. Your choices are based on how much you love yourself. THE MORE LOVE YOU DIRECT TO YOURSELF IN THE FORM OF LIGHT AND COLOR, THE MORE YOU "SEE" YOURSELF IN YOUR ENTIRETY - NOT JUST ONE LIFETIME OR ONE PERSONALITY, BUT AS A REFLECTING UNIVERSE CRADLED IN SAFETY AND LOVE.

Every second you have a choice. For some of you, this can be overwhelming and frightening because you don't know who you are. How can you make choices if you do not believe in your own power to do so — and do not believe in your safety while doing so? Many prefer to let others choose for them — to dream others' dreams — afraid to claim their own dream. In doing so, you produce a false harmony that affects the greater song. DARKNESS DOES NOT CREATE A FALSE HARMONY - IT IS YOUR CHOICE TO REJECT IT THAT DOES. ACCEPTANCE IS THE KEY THAT OPENS ALL DOORS, AND LOVE LIGHTS THE PATH.

YOU HAVE TO FIND YOUR COLORS -THEY ARE A ROADAP TO YOUR TRUTH. They take you to where you abandoned your dream and give you the chance to reclaim it. The signs are there pointing you in the direction you must go. Light is knowledge; and color is specific or unique knowledge. Think of it as looking up a word in the dictionary and finding the meaning of the word — or looking at a species and finding a particular example of that species. There are signs everywhere, but confusion is not necessary if you allow your own natural homing device to direct you to the paradigm that fits you. ILLNESS IS AN ATTEMPT TO DIRECT YOU; DEATH CAN DIRECT YOU, AND NOTHING IS AS PAINFUL AS RESISTING YOUR LIGHT AND COLOR. That is a death without life. You don't have to choose that kind of extermination; love does not desire it.

You are obsessed with objects that you "see" before you. Don't you realize they only appear solid in your realm. They serve as only to direct your attention or focus at the moment. YOUR SENSE OF WHAT YOU SEE ONLY HELPS YOU FOCUS, BUT DOES NOT PRESENT THE TRUE REALITY. Nothing is static or solid or permanent. What you see is a dream you can change in a heartbeat. The only requirement is to wake up to dream another dream. NO DREAM CAPTURES YOU UNLESS YOU AGREE TO THAT BONDAGE FOR THE PURIFICATION OF YOUR SOUL, AND DREAMS SPAWN REWARDS.

I had to ask, "How does emotion affect or determine light and color and fractals?

Kyalaka responds, *"Emotion is a signpost directing you to what needs attention. If you watch a movie, and you find yourself crying when the plot takes a turn, you have an opportunity to look at what you perceive as a tragedy or an injustice. The deeper you look into the emotion, you will discover a belief system that directs how you feel. The words e – motion points to its deeper meaning. It implies motion or movement. Therefore, your emotion moves you to awareness.* IF YOU SUPPRESS EMOTION; YOU SUPPRESS AWARENESS.

I ask, "Does emotion have color?"

Kyaklaka: *Absolutely – emotion is a frequency of light seen as a color ray. The nature or texture or speed of that ray indicates the intensity of that emotion or awareness. The emotion creates an environment in which that ray is expressed.*

Emotion can be dealt with on several levels. (1) It can be denied or rejected (2) It can be expressed in the moment or (3) It can be suppressed to be dealt with at a later date. The first is deadly; THE SECOND MOVES YOU TO HEALING; *the third sits in a dark place gathering dust or other values of color until it becomes a muddy brown. The more particles it collects through time, the denser the light. When you decide to pay attention to this "collection", you bring it forward as a dream long forgotten. The dream is muddy or unclear until you love it with your attention enough to bring it out of obscurity. WITHIN THAT DREAM ARE MEDICINES FOR YOUR AILMENT. There are potions that relieve the pain and sorrow. Light is being brought to your dream. The light is your own awareness and receive-ability. No emotion is beyond retrieve-ability, as long as you welcome it into your lives.*

Art therapy is the retrieval of emotions, dreams, and visions. ART THERAPY HEALS YOU AS THE COLORS, NEEDED FOR THAT HEALING, FLOCK AROUND YOU LIKE ANGELS. "Here I am" – they say. "I am that which you lost. I am that which you want to find again. I AM THAT WHICH HAS BEEN WAITING FOR YOUR ATTENTION. There are certain characteristics to colors on a general basis, but within each color is a value or FRACTAL depicting an individual story in a particular time and space. That value can indicate distance, degree of woundedness, and trigger mechanisms that brought this color to the forefront in this "now" moment.

"Can the colors heal with no intervention?" I ask.

THE COLORS THEMSELVES STIR THE EMOTIONS CONNECTED WITH THE WOUND. Then the person involved can either ignore the stirrings or begin to retrieve or heal those parts affected. For instance, a death in a past lifetime might have been traumatic – a hanging or drowning for instance. The residue of trauma can affect the present. Electrical circuits in the brain can produce colors that encode the trauma. When that arrangement of colors is duplicated in some way in the present, the person could electrically remember. The saving grace is that the person is no longer in that moment *of panic and can, by remembering, soothe the jolt to their psyche, and create a sense of wellbeing not experienced before. IF NOT ACCEPTED OR TRANSCENDED, THIS EVENT CAN **COLOR** ALL OTHER EXPERIENCE.*

February 24, 2000

~

Kyalaka, can you tell me more about light and love?

Love attracts the light. The light is that which must be seen in the moment. As the sun shines on one part of the globe, another part is in the dark. The shadows allow the spot light to illuminate a particular location or aspect of creation. All exists simultaneously. That which is the dark does not disappear – it only fades from outward recognition. It is hidden. The objects within the darkness feel their reality from within, not without, much like a spirit without a body. When that "spirit" loves, a light emanates outward into the darkness. That light attracts other lights like moths to a flame. Love is the essence of light. When a fire is fueled, it can not help but burn, and that burning creates more light.

WHEN AN ARTISTS PAINTS, HE FUELS THE FLAME. The colors are a description of the location of the light just as a star is a location point of the universe. You see a star – you judge its distance and size by the light it projects. If an artist paints darkly, he is perceiving in the dark an aspect that is not readily recognized or is so far away that it is barely detected. These aspects are detected much the way furniture is detected if one moved through a darkened bedroom. Other senses other than sight are used. Memory is used – where do I remember that chest of drawers was? You reach out with your hands and body to "touch" articles in your path. Pain is used when you stub your toe on the bedframe – oh, that's where that is. Anger at yourself for not remembering. Fear of falling or a dark force overcoming you in your vulnerability. Fear of being alone without assistance as if everything else can see but you. Questioning the very existence of this room in relation to what surrounds it. THIS IS THE ARTIST'S QUEST - TO SUBJECT HIMSELF TO THE DARKNESS IN ORDER TO FIND THE LIGHT WITHIN HIMSELF.

I interrupt, "Why can't the artist light the room and paint what he sees?

Kyalaka patiently explains. *The reason is that the eyes create illusion. The eyes tell you everything is in sight and close at hand. IT CAUSES YOU TO RELY ON WHAT YOU SEE - NOT WHAT YOU SENSE. It causes you to form an impression of reality based on an outside light source, but what if that light source changes location and direction? Then you have another reality.*

I did not trust outside light sources. Frankly, every time I followed an outside source, I got burned!!

Kyalaka continued. *Painting from an inside light source, the landscape may change, but your own personal light will reveal or fuel more light. In a sense, both are illusion because they are based on perceptions, but they are TWO DIFFERENT ROOMS. The artificial light reveals the objectification of "objects" whereas the inner light reveals the "life" in between the objects – the overlays of reality and dimension. The inner light is not dependent on "sight" but more on all the other senses you possess in order to perceive. To perceive is to "intuit" without having tangible proof. To "intuit" is to rely on more than the eyes or the brain, it involves the heart, mind, soul, spirit, and essentially every organ in the body to perceive reality. To "intuit" is to demand co-operation of all these body parts and aspects of soul and spirit. Since every part has a "story" to tell – a condensation is necessary to tell the comprised truth in the moment. Every part will have its day, but one painting is an agreement coming from the "whole." This "whole" marches and shines in its moment of glory. It is a moment which attracts other moments and other spirits, creating a "greater whole," thereby demonstrating the infinite manifestations of the fractal. THIS GREATER WHOLE IS EXPRESSED.*

I was trying to get an overview of these forces, so I asked, "What exactly is the love element in this stumbling through darkness?"

Kyalaka smiles and gathers her memory, determined to inform this eager student. Well, she says, courage is crucial because culture has great warnings and tragic depictions of this pursuit. Secrets are part of the darkness, and culture has created tremendous safeguards to protect secrets. Secrets are almost always designed to protect a select group of the whole. Parts that do not want to be seen for what they are. Parts that are pretending or presenting false appearances. Many have been killed so that secrets would not be told. So... to delve into the darkness carries a trepidation and tentativeness. Better to accept what is seen even if it is false, some say.

Kyalaka was aware she was not answering the question directly, but she was fairly confident that I would grab the ball and run with it.

"But what of truth?" I demanded. If truth needs no defending or no evangelical force, then why ever bring light to the darkness or expose the secrets? Personally, I always wanted to know where the furniture was in my darkened room. If I knew, I could then avoid the stubbed toe, the overwhelming fear, and the obstacles in my path. I could not "map-out" the truth for anyone else because they existed in other rooms, but I could help them with the process of recognizing the "signs." Why live in a false world when you could live in a true one. The only obstacle to the choice is "fear." What if the true one required something I did not possess?"

The answer almost came before I formed the question.

Kyalaka explained. *THE TRUE WORLD WILL NEVER REQUIRE ANYTHING YOU DON'T POSSESS OTHER THAN TO BE TRUE TO YOURSELF. Perhaps that alone is the greatest fear because you have been indoctrinated to believe that there is a great price to pay for that "privilege" and you fear being alone in your "truth." You have a lot of company in the "falseness." WHEN YOU ARE IN YOUR "FALSENESS," YOU ATTRACT THE SAME: WHEN YOU ARE IN YOUR TRUTH,*

YOU COLLECT AND ATTRACT OTHER LIGHTS WHO TRULY SUPPORT YOUR "STORY." Do you see the difference? SO TO BE IN YOUR PERSONAL TRUTH ATTRACTS A POWERFUL FORCE CALLED LOVE… A LOVE THAT ACCEPTS AND ENLIGHTENS.

If I dissected the word "en – light –en," I see that "light" is surrounded before and after with "en" or "in." I speculated that it could mean that a light "in" ourselves sparks a light "in" others. Love is the transmitter or mode of communication or locomotion.

I, in my skepticism, thought the above was indeed an interesting story, but I was faced with another story – the story that a darkness exists that will not receive or will reject any light. Did such a darkness truly exist? Scientists recently had defined a space in the cosmos as "dark energy." According to them, this space was immense. Was this space a trash bin or recycle bin of human/alien characteristics? Was it the space between words or the space between DNA? What function if any did this dark space serve? And was there any light in this darkness? I laughed at myself; I certainly knew how to ask questions. My computer programs were flooded with options.

Kyalaka interjected. The blackness is unformed potential. It exists as a backdrop against formed potential. Some call it evil, but it is simply life against itself. Light can only enter if there is a receiving factor. Life has the option to reject itself.

I asked, "Is there suffering involved?"

Why would there be suffering? Life that rejects itself is dead – no feeling.

But what of spirit?

Spirit is life.

Is there personality or essence?

No – unformed.

Is there a need to fear such darkness?

No – it is a choice.

Does it have influence over life?

Only if life chooses it.

What about the stories about the devil?

The d – evil is that part of us that chooses to not know ourselves.

Then does it have a force?

Absolutely.

Then does the dark have life?

Not in the sense you know it. The dark is disintegration of form.

Then what is spirit?

Spirit is disintegration of form in "light" or loosely-assembled form.

So the dark does not accept love?

Exactly.

So what if we try to love the darkness in an individual?

You can, but depending on the darkness, no response will be initiated.

Do we risk in such a love?

Only if you are expecting a response.

What is a black hole?

That which has collapsed into itself.

How does that relate to the above darkness?

Black holes are a stigmatism, so to speak. A problem with sight. The hole is not black, only not visible because of the speed of light at any given moment or location. There are worlds within worlds in black holes.

How does one handle all these unknown worlds?

You will know what you need to know when you need to know it. Otherwise, you will be overloaded with non-essential information. If you are exploring the landscape in Africa, information about Connecticut could be distantly related but not imminently pertinent.

CHAPTER 41

Love Heals

Love is a coagulator, an enzyme, that brings elements together.

Mya, of course, still wondered about this thing called "love." How in the world could she bring this element into her work, her passion. She posed the question, and words began to form in her mind. She wrote:

That on which you focus your attention is changed and in turn changes you. Love is respectful attention. Hate is disrespectful attention.

Love is a coagulator, an enzyme, that brings elements together to meet, discuss, relate, and mediate. In the body, blood coagulates or clots. Without this coagulation, the body would bleed to death. In life, love coagulates. In places of imbalance, this love focuses on issues and resolve by bringing together the necessary healing elements. Disease, trauma, defining moments, death all have a way of directing traffic in a congested intersection.

Respect is a crucial ingredient for favorable results. If the approach is aimed at annihilation or to get rid of (in the case of disease) the larger picture is not seen, and shallow results or perceptions are acquired. In a sense, love refracts. In other words, love does not reflect to one source but refracts to many parts, allowing more healing and more conclusive impact.

With this approach or insight, she looked at her Van Gogh experience and all of her painting journeys. The paintings themselves were only the beginning, the open door, or the cut into the wound. Once the colors or sources of light were revealed in a topographical map, love was necessary to coat or stitch up the wound. Mya wondered if this was why the sand in a healing ceremony was scattered afterwards to release the spirits. Sometimes she felt that some paintings had not been stitched up or coagulated but were still bleeding. Sometimes she had to paint the borders of the paintings a certain color to feel as if the energy was "sealed" or contained within a proper boundary.

As a little girl, Mya's sand castles were explorations into the ways things "settled" or fell away into the depths… the layering of "sand worlds" and the deeper layering of "human experience." All she was aware of as a child was that this playing in the sand brought her great joy and a feeling of safety. That world existed only for her and her love. Respect was present in this relationship. Respect formed a partnership in creating beautiful landscapes of the mind. Nothing compared to this love relationship – not even the love Mya felt for her family. Perhaps she was autistic in a sense – loving and living in her own world, but she felt blessed, not handicapped. Others could enter her world, but only if they said the magic words, "open, sesame." If they disrespected the creations, the door slammed shut, and no magic word would thence open the door again. Perhaps she was selfish in shutting others out, but she could see no happy ending if certain rights were not honored.

Mya was still building her sand castles in the sky – still opening wounds, and stitching up – still traveling to some distant star to see who lived there – still hovering over her creations, protecting them as her children – still sifting and shifting the sands of time, rearranging the past, present, and future – and still loving what she birthed. Her creations changed her, healed her, and coagulated her life experience. So far few dared to say the magic words, and she was sad about that, but time would open the proper doors. When the time was right, the cat would meow at the door, and she would put out fresh food and water to welcome the hungry cat.

In regard to Van Gogh, the cat did meow at her door. Her love and respect for the Van Gogh life inspired her to create new landscapes out of the "old sand." By cathexis,[22] the concentration of psychic energy, she brought healing and a "lighted" understanding of many dark places. Van Gogh was no longer bleeding.

---

22 *"the concentration of psychic energy on some particular person, thing, idea, or aspect of the self* - Webster's New World Dictionary

CHAPTER 42

Beauty Transforms

- Archangel Michael -
Beauty is a sacred mantra.

SEPTEMBER 3, 2001

To comprehend beauty is to make a connection to an underlying rhythm of form. BEAUTY SPEAKS OF THE HEART - REVEALS ESSENCE - TRANSCENDS IDEOLOGY. Beauty can be found in violence, in a gnarled tree branch, and in sheer ugliness. Beauty is truth in the way that "many" represents "one." When we (as humans) recognize the common denominator in beauty, we recognize its many forms. Without beauty, we are soulless mannequins. WITH beauty we become alive and hopeful of "utopia."

When I try to create ugliness, beauty is there. When I try to create "a happy picture," melancholy is there. One does not always seek beauty, but one is nevertheless overcome by beauty, unaware of how it managed to make itself known. Beauty happens when we perceive a truth whether it is in victimhood or sainthood… no difference. Beauty rarely shows itself in sentimental drivel. It will, however, show itself when the true nature of a thing is revealed. Beauty is present in fantasy only in the sense that fantasy is true to imagination. Beauty is present in squalor only in the sense that it reminds us nothing is static, always changing from integration to disintegration, and ALL IS SACRED. Smells can be beautiful from the smell of a rose to the smell of garbage. These smells remind us of timely blossoming and joyful releasing of that which has outlived its time. Beauty has a place in temporal reality and also spiritual reality. Beauty stands before us yanking at our sensibilities, demanding to be heard, felt, and seen.

Beauty feeds our bodies, our souls, our spirits. It can make us melancholy as our soul remembers the loss of love, even a love imagined. It can remind us of a purity in an impure world; thereby again reminding us of a sense of loss. Most of us want to "freeze" this kind of beauty and clutch it to our breasts, encapsulating it, as if putting money in the bank for a rainy day.

Beauty represents a type of security - a method by which we tolerate and endure those supposed hardships and woundings. It transcends and transforms our reality in the way that the higher self reminds us we are much more than we can ever imagine. Beauty expands us and opens us, sometimes allowing the arrows of recognition to pierce our hearts. It transcends cultural likes and dislikes and responds more to transitory moments than to established norms in any time period. It does not have a race or creed, but rather a commonality of humanness.

Beauty is connected to understanding. Pain can be beautiful in the way that tragedy can be enlightening. Beauty brings us to our knees, creating an egoless humility. By whatever means beauty shows itself, it transforms us and transmutes the poison of mediocrity and drudgery. It puts a spark in our eye, a love in our hearts, and a liveliness in our steps. At that moment when we touch the unknowable, the unknowable has a chance to know us. That communion sustains and enriches us beyond belief. "A rose by any other name is still a rose," as "beauty by any other name is still beauty." We insist on labeling or naming beauty, while beauty extends itself in limitless forms. May I always "feel" beauty and live in eternal gratitude for the privilege.

AND BEAUTY HEALS!!!!

> The Soul speaks Beauty;
> The Spirit dances Beauty;
> *And the Human must perpetuate Beauty -*
> *All from the Breath of Heaven.*
> ~ Archangel Michael ~

Author Ken Carey speaks of an "indigenous consciousness" in his books and relays his ideas about beauty by saying, "You are the love of the Creator embodied in human form."... "You are here in the service of universal art to create beauty..."... "the evocation of beauty and the description of truth" - this is the purpose of life and the universe.[23]

Van Gogh loved nature, and to me, this "nature" was the creation of the Creator. He said:
"If you truly love nature, you will find beauty everywhere."[24]

> I AM
> The Angel of Land and Sea

---

23 *The Return of the Bird Tribes* by Ken Carey, p. 208.
24 Vol. I, p. 20.

My wings reflect the creations in the waters and the formations on the land and the Earth in space. My essence opens your eyes to the marvels of creation and your oneness with All That Is. Opening to the magnificence, you are supported and transported into a <u>REALM OF BEAUTY.</u>

Message from The *- Angels -*
Beauty follows a path directed by spirit, a path to the heart. It expands your capacity to love, your capacity to heal, to remember. Beauty is in the eye of the Beloved.

As I reflected on the concept of beauty, I remembered how I first chose Sheweia as my artist name. I only know that the name was created out of necessity to stand my ground, to define myself amidst all the confusion and the names spoken by others that did not speak to me - that did not embrace the completeness of me. To create it, I had a vision of a little girl riding on an elephant, and feeling tones began to wash over me. I started uttering sounds that resonated with me, that spoke to my soul, that made me feel beautiful, special, loved, and cherished - God's name for me. Later I wondered if the name reflected my higher self who had a place on the other side, who was close to the God energy. And when I dissected the name, I realized it encompassed the totality in human terms. She - the feminine He - the masculine We - the collective I-the divinity and A - the human soul.

The name flowed like water, like the embracing arms of the Mother energy - comforting, soothing, and melodic and yet solid and unshakable, unmovable. I thought of the name as Ancient, as representing the Goddess, the Divine Feminine and so much more that words could not touch.

Someone once told me that the name meant "She who walks in beauty." And I actually found a poem written by Lord Byron called "She Walks in Beauty."

"She walks in beauty, like the night
Of cloudless climes and starry skies:
And all that's best of dark and bright
Meet in her aspect and her eyes
Thus mellow's\d to that tender light
Which heaven to gaudy day denies."....

His words seemed to partially touch what Sheweia represented. As Sheweia, I was not just the light but also the dark.

In the poem by Lord Byron,... "if she were to have even one shade more darkness, or a bit less light, she would be, though not wholly ruined, "half impair'd"...[25] And I thought of a starry, starry night where the beautiful, shining stars could not be seen if not for the deep indigo sky.

I had no idea at the time of the power involved, but I am getting a glimpse now. I was calling in beauty, acceptance, and peace. "I AM SHEWEIA." MY SOUL REJOICES. In 1980 I created that which would go forth in time to heal all my fragmented soul parts. I spoke VICTORY into my life. I could actually HEAR the sound of my wholeness and perfection. "I AM THAT WHICH I AM BECOMING."

---

25 www.poetryfoundation.org/poem/173100.

CHAPTER 43

Aborted Dreams

Seven Generations

Even though my name gave me so much power and confidence, all was not "light." The harvest time that Vincent spoke of seemed so far from actuality. I had to put it aside for a while. In the meantime, I worked feverishly to have a special gallery opening revealing many of my discoveries. The gallery had "Vincent" all over it from paintings done in Van Gogh strokes to decor that reflected his colors. I was so proud of being able to pull together this exhibit to reveal what I had discovered. Preceding the show I underwent unimaginable painful and energy-draining processes. I was panting up to the finish line of an enormous marathon of challenges. So as I laid it out for all to see, I was recovering, but still weak from the fight.

I looked for signs of recognition from the gallery visitors and, for the most part, found none. Perhaps words unspoken would have revealed another story. However, one lady came up to me and began asking me to talk about the paintings. I said something about in healing Van Gogh I had healed myself; tears filled her eyes and I could tell "she got it." She matched the vibration and saw the true picture underneath the plastic paint. What a moment!

But after the show I fell into a depression, feeling impotent at expressing what I felt compelled to express, and feeling devoid of hope that the dream of reaching others would ever materialize. It was a dream that could not breathe or find the space to grow. What was the point? I had not sold anything at the show, and I had rent to pay for the studio and my home.

I was exhausted and couldn't seem to find the energy to drive to the studio and work. I would get there, prepare to work, and then I would get hungry or just not be inspired to begin. I decided part of the problem was that all my paintings were stored in the place I painted. Ghosts lined up and stacked against the walls seemed to weight me down. I would lock up and go home again and again.

What was I handing down? I thought of the Native American teaching about seven generations… that when we heal we heal seven generations before and seven generations after. How was this possible now? The link seemed severed, and the dream dead.

September 11, 2001

⤳

Then 9-11 happened and other concepts of reality fell. The rent went up on my studio space, and I couldn't find the energy to open the door to the studio and find the motivation to move forward. Nothing made sense anymore. I didn't renew the lease on the studio and I prepared a small room at home to serve as a studio.

I painted a few paintings after that but never acquired any strong foundation to build another dream. My body could no longer stand up to bat. WHATEVER NEEDED TO COME THROUGH WAS EITHER TOO HEAVY OR TOO LIGHT TO GET PAST MY RESISTANCE.

Message from Archangel Michael -Sheweia, Sheweia, Sheweia, you are so dear with your never-ending attempt to understand. You did nothing wrong. In a way, your anger kept you alive, but now you don't need it anymore. You can finally let go and forgive yourself for your "perceived shortcomings or failures. You did not fail; you were just in a dream that could not ACTUALIZE IN "REALTIME." You were never alone - you just walled yourself in with your perception of reality. You can breathe now: you have pecked through the stones and "stories" holding the wall, and you can see the light on the other side. We love you and celebrate you in all your glorious human-ness, your unstoppable spirit, and your willingness to listen. (2014)

CHAPTER 44

The Child Remembers the Dream

She giggles as she skips through fields of gold.

Mya writes: The field of psychology has many labels and diagnoses to explain human behavior and psychosis, but many times the underlying truth and complexity of who we are is missed. These labels often lead to medicines and treatments that often destroy the mystery of the soul and its aims. On the other hand, I think the human being has the ability to become one with any idea, ability, person, or historical event – that perceiving outside time or in "no time," one can touch the past, present, future - not only individually, but collectively. IF WE HAVE THAT ABILITY TO BECOME "ONE WITH"; THEN PERHAPS WE ARE INDEED "ONE."

I have no doubt that I somehow have expanded my experience to include Van Gogh, Michelangelo, and others, and that "touching" or caring enough to pay attention to or observe their lives actually changed them as well as me. In spite of so many lives and missions and goals – I was drawn to certain past lives that influenced me in the present. The adventure was not a fantasy, but one rooted in reality and the here and now. To give way to such memories and adventures is a response to a broader and more expansive view of reality. Such memories can overwhelm, but such memories can also enrich and enlighten and heal. To give yourself permission to open the door is a gift. No one will give you a map – the key to the door can't be picked up at the local hardware store. YOU only have the key. Curiosity will take you over the threshold, and the other side will be "lighted" for your particular viewing. Have a wonderful journey!!!!!

JOURNAL:

All of my life I have been the observer, watching, waiting. I watched as I witnessed the world's antics. Most of it made no sense to me. I sometimes thought that a spaceship had dropped me off on earth and had forgot to come and pick me up.

Here on Earth, I found madness in the most solid of structures, and jewels in the most crazy of structures. Since I didn't know the earth was a grand play or production where roles were donned and discarded constantly, I tried to figure out my script among changing environments and atmospheres. I had no idea what my lines were, and as a result, I tripped on other's lines. I finished their sentences and assumed their intent was mine. I created their dialogues as a prompt for me to remember my own lines. I had one jewel – I WAS DETERMINED TO FIND MY VOICE.

First, I had to shed the guilt and shame of having such a wish, since confidence was not in the water I drank as a child or a strong healthy ego in the food I ate. I "sat" on my observation that I was different, and that my ideas were stray puppies trying to find a home. So I waited. I couldn't seem to go along with the concept of God I found around me, and I was still very allergic to that virus "shame." I realized that I was considered "wrong," but I just couldn't change the way I felt. And every time I put on the mask of belonging, I lost so much energy that I had to take it off again. I couldn't live the dream of others, and the colors were not the same. I learned that the colors lost their light unless they were mine. My pursuit conflicted with my parents' dream. Their perception of God told them that I was on the wrong path and the truth I felt I touched was only a figment of my imagination or worse still the Devil. In some way, my programming encouraged me to live their dream in order to please them; I truly wanted to do so because I wanted them to be happy and content – but you see, every time I painted the colors of their dream – the colors lost their light, and the muddiness made me sick.

Light is true to its course; it will not beam unless it finds its mark. When I painted, I tried to paint with colors designed for others. Finally deep within me arose my true colors. Then, in a flash, light's beam touched me, and I was that child again – <u>INNOCENT OF THE WORLD'S DREAM.</u> Layers and layers of do's and don'ts peeled away. Layers and layers of dogma and tradition peeled away, and I became the "seeded" dreams of my own making. I became visible and legitimate.

I tried to "go along" with many dreams, but THE LIE WOUNDED ME. Until clarity came to my personal truth, I was not attracting the pure beams of light designed to find their mark. I was not attracting those who would recognize the light – others with similar dreams.

When clarity came, out of time and space came two beams of light – Van Gogh and Michelangelo. Our personal dreams were color and form dancing in the sands of time, forming the landscape of future hills and valleys. Spirit touched our dreams, and grace gave us the power to be Gods and Goddesses. The blend of our soul parts were given the wings of the eagle to overcome ego's illusion. A part of the eagle is humbled, still remembering not being able to leave the nest, and then he spreads his wings and leaps, feeling the wind catch his wings.

But when we see with the eagle's eyes, we sense the grander vision, and we forgive ourselves and others for our defective sight, our astigmatism and myopic vision, for those things that are blurred from sight. Forgiveness means giving before knowing the whole truth. It is having faith that a true story exists under the illusion – that all dreams can have a part in this story. Not being able to for – give is to invalidate the eagle's sight – to invalidate your purpose in the landscape of the higher mind. Without love, one can't accept the underlying story. Without love, your lines are read in isolation with no connection to the other players. You are alone on stage with no props or lines to which to respond or react. You don't even have the advantage of a spot light - no light – no color. You are in the dark, and the director and audience are no where to be found.

I felt my confusion melt away and my heart was filled with love for my parents and all the other players in the cast. The word for – giveness made sense for the first time in my life Forgiveness had nothing to do with the words I had heard in countless dogmas. Forgiveness comes from the e – motion of moving with the element of trust and "not knowing"… not relying on some "other," but believing in your own worth in creation, in your own ability to create and to deliver your words with strength and purpose. I didn't have to play all the other parts – only to play my own with conviction and joy. I WAS NOT REQUIRED TO BE ANYTHING BUT THAT WHICH I WAS. Simple. The training may take lifetimes, but when the words, colors, and light came – I knew. No shyness, no stuttering, no hesitation. I was in my safe place.

Message from The ~ angels ~
The world is in divine order, all vibrating to love's chime. (2013)

CHAPTER 45

Post-Traumatic Stress

"We are the ones we've been waiting for."[26]

Triggers and symbols impede and infringe on my "normal day-to-day living like a virus disrupting the software on a computer. I see a gun on TV and I catapult into a scenario of circumstances and emotional turmoil far removed from the actual scene. I react violently against what is all too familiar in my memory. I see a barbed wire fence, and I am filled with horror. The re-occurring image of a giant hook sends shivers up my spine, and I am haunted by the farmhouse of my childhood. I am there in my night and waking dreams, terrorized by I know not what.

These flashbacks, surrounded by confusion and unanswered questions, began around 1980 and intensified their presence thereafter, telling me there was something I did not know or remember about this time. I indulged them, ignored them, and pushed at them to reveal the truth. Nothing in what I was told about my childhood supported the feelings and emotions I was experiencing. No outside force or person could tell me what I had forgotten. I was left with all of the emotion, but none of the "so-called facts." I tried every psychological and spiritual approach conceivable. In one of these sessions, I had a vision:

I am a little girl dressed in a pinafore with many petticoats underneath. I am standing behind a glass in a room much like the rooms in a police station designed for victims to identify aggressors anonymously. I recognized the perpetrator, but I did not want to identify him. I knew my identification would shock and change lives. But then, I forced myself to stare into the face behind the glass, and I saw no feeling, no emotion, no recognition or awareness in that face. In that moment I knew I had to tell the truth, not for him (because the truth would not change his deadness) but for me who could not live with this terrible burden. So I identified him.

---

26 "The Collected Poems of June Jordan," 2005.

This session was obviously some metaphor for what haunted me, but it was not the end-all to the surfacing of some unrest. The farmhouse continued to pull me back, and when the feelings of terror would overwhelm me, my guides and angels would pull me out. Their exact words were, "Get her out of there." My connection with spirit, taught through shamanism, enabled many journeys to facilitate healing. I worked at letting go of the shame, not my own, healing the inner child, breaking any past contracts, and learning and accepting my personal truth.

Mya, in her insistence on healing, found herself lying on a floor in a medicine woman's home. She had requested a soul retrieval, common in shamanistic practices. The idea was that we lose fragments of ourselves when we are in trauma or in a situation that is unacceptable to our frame of reference. When these pieces leave, they carry that which is not desired but also the positive side or potential of the characteristics involved. Therefore, when we reject the experience, we reject the power inherent and the medicine needed to heal. The soul part resides elsewhere until the person can integrate. A medicine woman facilitates this retrieval and integration.

So Mya feels a sensation as the medicine woman "blows" the soul part back into her body. She rises to drink water and begin to come forth out of the ritual. She looks around with childlike wonder and with a body that feels like rubber… no tension or aches or stiffness almost to the point of not being able to walk.

The medicine woman tells her what she experienced and what happened. She found Mya's 5 year old soul part sitting in the dirt in a shed. The medicine woman told her that it was time to go home and that Sheweia was waiting for her. She agreed to go back. Half way through the process, she insisted on going back to retrieve her dolly. Although the doll was covered in mud, the operation was a success.

I, as an adult, after the soul retrieval, felt compelled to integrate that soul part by going to the store and buying a new baby doll dressed in an old-fashioned flowered smock. I wanted to care for that little girl within and integrate her back into my life. I wanted to provide a safe place for her so she wouldn't have to leave again.

Something caused the fracture to begin with and I spent fifty years searching for the answers. At one point I underwent acupuncture, hoping to relieve what haunted me. I awoke later after the treatment in the middle of the night terrified – I was huddled again in the corner of that house. I first came to the conclusion that it didn't matter what happened there – what did matter was that whatever it was – it was powerful enough to FRAGMENT MY PSYCHE. In that moment

I decided I had to believe and honor and love that little girl like never before. The terror was real, the fragmentation was real, and the impact was real.

Then a year later when I had my confrontation with the sacred knife, considering just leaving this world, the threads of defining moments began weaving a tighter strand. Issues of abandonment, lies, secrets, and betrayal compounded into a gigantic ball of yarn. Time had no significance; it was the same movie, and it was part of many others' movies.

For some, post-traumatic stress is identified with war, and those experiencing this type know that the flashbacks can continue for years, changing their lives forever. But what of flashbacks from other lives lived? Could not the trauma be constantly reinforced throughout lifetimes until the psychic energy is released? I, for one, believe this is so.

As my psyche began to heal after contemplating ending my life in 2000, I was given another opportunity in spirit to truly leave if I wanted to die. But at that time I had healed and integrated enough to reply, "No." I wanted to stay. I was strong enough to continue and to accept the challenge to embrace life, and my wish was granted.

And the farmhouse? In shamanic journeys I found myself there again and again to confront or discover what energy was there. To heal, I followed psychological and spiritual avenues of visualizing the building being disintegrated before my eyes. I raged enough to break out windows, to provide avenues of escape. In 2001, in a visualization, I tore down more of the structure with the help of spirit, angels, and guides. Even when no walls were visible, I wanted to do more - I needed to do more. I needed to see it all gone - all the energy that sucked the very life out of me. My wish was granted. Then in a split second I saw the corner of the house as before, but I was no longer there. In my place of terror was a glass of water with one fresh daisy calmly and sweetly standing tall. Peace filled my heart, and it was finally over, at least I thought so at the time.

When my lover left in 2000, and the door softly shut, shockwaves across time sent a tidal wave. The pattern in the weaving became so clear and strong that I saw how the design must be changed. I unraveled the past to create the future.

Later I wondered how I could help others with my story. If only those who have lived similar lives could read this and release some of their isolation, pain, and distrust of self and see <u>HOW CREATIVITY AND LOVE CAN CHANGE EVERYTHING.</u>

Shock has a way of waking you up from a collective dream. You realize that things are not as you supposed. SHOCK CAN PULL YOU OUT OF THE LIES TOLD TO YOU AND BY YOU, AND THE ENERGY YOU GAIN CAN BE DIRECTED TOWARD YOUR PERSONAL TRUTH WITH POWER AND CLARITY. When the house has collapsed, you can begin rebuilding with more durable materials and updated knowledge. You can build on solid rock that is your core, and your windows can be open, letting your spirit flow from room to room. If others destroy the house, you can always rebuild because you have the <u>true blueprint.</u> The doors are in the right places, and you have the key to open and close them at will. You now have the power over your own life and destiny. You have conquered the faceless enemy and saboteur of your joy. When the door softly closes, you will be able to OPEN OTHER DOORS OUTSIDE TIME AND SPACE AND ENTER THE SACRED THAT BRINGS YOU HEALING AND WHOLENESS AND ENCOURAGES YOUR LONG AWAITED VICTORY. My hope is that others will find their joy, and love will heal their experienced wounds, and they will realize their perfection and their "wholeness." or their "holiness."

I AM

The Angel of Transcendence

I help you rise above your concerns and worries. My lavender color maps the way to higher thoughts and visions. My love transports you to a higher plane where you can feel how loved and cherished you are by the most High God.

Message from Sheweia/Angels
*Bless the wound that jolts you out of who you thought you were into discovering who you really are. Bless all that **painted** the picture of your rise and fall.* (2013)

CHAPTER 46

The Real Me

I called my name, and I answered.

APRIL 2013

～

Here I am, about 15 years later. I am living in my home state, answering the call of a new generation, my grandchildren. I take my job seriously, wondering what I have to give to them - what I will be passing on to them. I wanted to "clean up my act" and have the knowledge of my ancestry so that I could consciously give them the best I had.

I know I made the right decision, but I feel alienated in this geographical location, which is my birth home, but not my spiritual home.

I had lost the colors again; slowly before I moved and then I just couldn't pull them up again in my new location. I hadn't painted and could barely sketch a few drawings (an exploration tracing my ancestry). Remembering how my body had shut down when I had painted before, I knew I was not physically or psychically able to sustain the process. So I waited, busying myself with researching my history and that of the German people. I researched the World Wars and how artists were affected by Hitler's decisions. All this time, I mourned for that side of myself that was imprisoned - that side I could not touch. Reminders surfaced from time to time, remembering the intensity and the emotion of painting, of accomplishing never-imagined feats of expansion. I realized I was living a whole new life. My life now was more secure and safe?, but nevertheless more soul-less and subdued. I was not risking; I was maintaining. I was not fiercely passionate; I was kind and considerate. (smiling)

Then some project, idea, or curiosity drove me to drag out my old journals to get a sense of where I had been and where I was going. As I read, I realized how much I had buried. Such pain and sorrow, such searching for answers, and such revelation and wisdom flowing from my finger tips, unbeknownst to my conscious mind. I would read entries where some beautiful and peaceful solution was reached and written down, but the absorption would only happen in time clips over the many years following. I had heard the expression, "If I only knew then what I know now." Well I <u>DID</u> know it then - at least it had made its presence known.

Affirmation: I am on a divine mission, and I am speaking in my power voice.

What also was known to me through the writing was a horrific and painful language describing some trauma. The words cut through my perceived persona, dispelling what I thought I knew about myself. The words were relentless and the emotion was heart-wrenching. The handwriting changed, sometime almost illegible, since I wrote with my left hand to bypass my dominant thoughts. The impact of the words were familiar and yet alien to my sensibilities.

Seeing how many times the passages surfaced over the years, I was forced, as never before, to consider the validity and truth and relevancy. Why would this material keep surfacing over and over? What would I do with the realization NOW? Should I bury it or burn it? I actually tore some from the journals, simply because the picture was too dark. I called in my guides, my power animals, love itself. I then prayed, smudged, meditated, wrote words of forgiveness, and tore the papers into little bits, putting them in a coffee can, and burning them in the back yard, releasing the "charged" words. I wept, coming to terms with what I had carried, and the unbelievable strength and courage I must have had to go forward - NOT ONLY TO GO FORWARD, BUT TO CONTINUE SEEKING THE TRUTH.

I was <u>shocked!</u> It was always here right before my eyes! I read my own words on the page, but still could not let the implications into my psyche. I guess I always existed in some limbo state of half believing and not believing....self-trust was virtually impossible. "If I didn't know the truth about this one thing: I didn't know the truth of any other."

Today I finally realize that such a wound seriously undermines your ability to have confidence in yourself, in what you're doing - your place in the world. It undermines everything you touch. The insecurity permeates every decision, every action, every deed. <u>To have such a deep wound and not have it visible or even believed cripples you beyond belief.</u> What I didn't know was that if one person or spirit outside of yourself validates your wound, and you believe them, <u>EVERYTHING IN YOUR WORLD CHANGES.</u>

Many years ago, by a river and a waterfall, I was meditating, and I felt the presence of the Archangel, Michael. I had journaled and somehow he was a part of my life then, but AGAIN, I questioned whether what I was receiving was REAL, just like the amazing shamanic journeys I had taken. So I took my regular pose of believing and not believing.

JULY, 2012

Almost 10 months ago, I was frustrated about why I had not gotten my artwork out into the public like I hoped… so I went for a reading from a friend of a friend. The reading seemed to take a turn into what I needed to leave behind from my old life that didn't serve me. Now ARCHANGEL MICHAEL came forward again, and I felt that presence again. Somehow I felt that Michael knew me like no other….that I was OK, that I could be "myself." That day he validated that the pain-filled feelings and experiences I had written in my journal were indeed true - not made up. I almost fell on the floor with release, relief, and confirmation. My life, in my heart, suddenly took a different shape, a brighter color, a Light that could not be extinguished. What he said to me changed my life forever - it was as if love stepped through the door and greeted me. My heart could hardly contain the energy. But this time, I knew it was REAL.

Now as I create my art, I trust in an on-going INTENT made in my sacred circle, but if I get "stuck" or the design is not flowing freely, I think of Michael, and he is there. I create and he supports and uses his vibration to root me in the "divine on earth."

After the reading, my heart always seemed to be breaking or my emotions overflowing, and then I thought maybe my heart was instead opening and being drenched with the well-spring of tenderness.

Events and emotions from the past would surface, and I would be pounded by the force, seeing myself in the "primal scream," echoing out into a dark space. Then my thoughts would go to Michael, to the divine feminine, to the Divine Mother and in a instant the wave would pass, and I would be left sitting on the beach in the sand, quiet and relaxed. In the past I confronted these emotions and gave my body over to release them, but I was drained for days, and I felt alone. Today, "someone" was always standing by.

Message from - *Archangel Michael* -
We have been holding and loving you for a long, long time.

I began my relationship with Michael through the reading, and I began my relationship with the Divine Mother through seeking her out in the approaching 2013 Mayan Ending and Beginning, where it was prophesied that the feminine would be healed and heal, bringing about balance between the feminine and masculine. I implored her to heal and bless my family, but first, I prayed,

"Divine Mother, we are grateful for your presence in our lives. We honor you and welcome your warm embrace, your love and caring. We feel your support, your nurturing, your sustenance. We thank you for blessing our lives, and extending them into the fullest expression of love. We feel your arms around us, holding us in divine grace. Blessings!

Thereafter I seemed to be releasing periodically, not in a heavy way, but lightly and swiftly with no residue. My life, hope, and dreams had been shared with Spirit for many, many years, but the time had come for a "new story."

I AM
The Angel of Transformation
Like the caterpillar transforms into the butterfly, you are transforming into your Highest Self. Your heaviness is dropping away like baser metals turning into gold. You are becoming transparent as you lift your wings to fly, but you will always remember the ground of your existence as you put on different guises and play different roles.
YOU ARE LOVE!!!

APRIL 4, 2013

I woke up, trying to remember a dream. I checked my facebook page, and there was a post about "dragonfly." It talked about dragonfly being the "Keeper of Dreams." Somehow in all the study with power animals over the dreams, the "dream" part had not stuck in my memory, and now here it was. I checked my book on Medicine Cards by Jamie Sams, pp. 144-45, and I saw the words "illusion and transformation." Dragonfly - "...breaks illusions, brings visions of power, no need to prove it."[27]

I had become powerless, caught in the reflections of others and their dreams; I couldn't find the power in "the real me." I believed I was the mask I wore.

---

27 "Medicine Cards" by Jamie Sams, p. 144-45.

I suddenly remembered my "Sacred Knife," the one mentioned in the first chapter. Before painting, I always established my sacred circle, called in my guides and power animals, and held the knife high over my head, declaring:

I am cutting through the veils of illusion, finding my way to the truth of who I am.

Maybe that knife was indeed a very, very sacred tool. Aho!

CHAPTER 47

Patchwork

.... pieces of truth ....

APRIL 28, 2013

I am stumbling toward the bathroom when out of nowhere? came a memory of a family gathering that took place around 1950:

I am under my grandpa's drafting table, being VERY still, hardly breathing. My cousins and I are playing hide-and-seek.

The game was intense, at least to me, and I didn't want to be found. I was well aware that being alone in this place was my "safe spot." I felt more secure alone here than with my cousins and relatives.

I didn't know then why, but now I feel that these were my sacred moments growing up, moments in which I wasn't overwehlmed by other stories and other versions of the truth. Alone I believed I was in my purest state: their stories could not touch me, and I knew who I was.

Telling my stories in this book is perhaps the first time I have consistently come out from under that table. I now know I have a right to my story, and the Divine has a use for it. No one of us knows the full story of their particular soul - all we can do is "piece" together glimpses of the truth. To not tell the story because it is incomplete or because part of us cannot absorb our own story or because we are afraid is the temptation - the temptation that keeps us in bondage... to keep quiet, having the mistaken notion that we are protecting someone or something or that our voice does not matter. However, the PATCHWORK QUILT will not be complete until we have all the stories. A hole will remain - and the threads will be severed connecting our stories as a human species. My story may light a dark patch in your story; just as others will. The beauty and warmth of the quilt depends on it.

I AM

The Angel of Mystic Mountain

I hold the mystery of the universe. I am the totem for the fabric of your lives,
the threads that connect you to the mountain spirits. In me and through me,
you feel the spirit of the animals and of all creation. You are a patchwork of
seen and unseen, and my compass helps you root in ALL THAT IS.

I can't write your story or know how it weaves with my story until I add the stitches. Like my Mother used to say, "the stitches have to be small and close together." Maybe that is to insure that no truth will lose its uniqueness within the whole - that we are bound together by our common spirit and the Divine Feminine that birthed us. I think we are all "seeds of greatness" sprouting out of the rich heritage of soul memories, coming together to create a new world based on the truth and a beauty unimaginable.

This truth and beauty will birth new patterns of color and light and magnificence, and WE WILL REMEMBER WHO WE ARE.

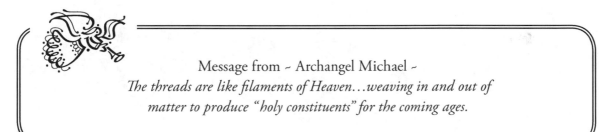

Message from ~ Archangel Michael ~
The threads are like filaments of Heaven…weaving in and out of
matter to produce "holy constituents" for the coming ages.

I can no longer hide under the table.

CONCLUSION

As fallen angels, we return to earth's path to heal

"THE MOTHER."

I reflected on the soul's journey and how color and light were an integral part of such a journey. I reflected on my journey across time and space, represented by the door opening and closing. I reflected on how I, Van Gogh, and Michelangelo entered the present by healing the traumas of the past. I reflected on what I had learned about reflective properties - gold, silver, copper, crystal and the power of sacred tools - the sacred knife, the red shawl, and the sacred circle. Now I needed to tell the world how to heal with color, how to work with light, and how to forgive.

Kyalaka, my higher self, was standing by, so I asked:

Mya: What do people need to know about color?

Kyalaka: *Color is the tangible substance by which they can reach other realms within themselves. WHAT THE EYE SEES IS A STEPPING STONE TO WHAT THE HEART FEELS. Listen to what creates an emotional response. Dialogue with the color to find its message to you. Know that the spectrum of light can travel great distances across time to bring to you that which you have lost and forgotten.*

When you retrieve those parts of yourselves lost in time, you finally arrive at the present moment where anything is possible. YOU FINALLY GET YOUR WINGS - YOUR FORGOTTEN HERITAGE. Those wings are your freedom - the ability to respond from your core to any given situation.

JUDGMENTS ABOUT RIGHT AND WRONG ARE SHADOW BELIEFS ABOUT NOT KNOWING WHO YOU ARE. Judgment is a control-based system designed to clip your wings. It offers a false security for those who do not feel their wings or suffer from cracked to bleeding wings. YOU WERE NEVER MEANT TO FORGET WHO YOU WERE. It was a lie you believed - the lie became your reality.

Color helps you remember because color contains within itself the "lighted message" of your birthright. Gather your colored eggs and explore each one with joy and respect. Live your life as if the Gods and Goddesses were on your side helping you remember. There is no time, only the power of experience.

Mya: What can people do if they have not chosen to be an artist? How can they work with color to heal?

Kyalaka: *Do you not all live with color and light each day? What color car do you prefer? What kind of bulbs do you buy for your lamps? What color clothes do you wear? Every choice is one in which you direct your destination - your ship to the stars. Every choice (if you follow your preferences) is a chance to remember. Become one with the color and be willing to experience the emotion. Be willing to hear the voices from the past and the future. Be willing to slip through the crevices of time to the eternal NOW.*

Honor your artists who help you remember. Sound, too, is a color; so honor your musicians and singers. Stories are sounds, also; so honor your storytellers. Everything you see, hear, or touch, is a color, a vibration of light.

Open your senses - you will know. Open your heart - and you will finally feel. Open your mind - and you will think from the Higher mind. Open your soul, and you will realize all fragments come from one complete whole. Open your spirit, and you will heal your broken wings. The "other" for which you long are your fragmented parts. The "other" is what your soul remembers. The "other" is your nemesis waiting to be forgiven.

I reflected how the story began with that door opening and closing and the cat meowing. What did it all mean on the basest of levels?

Kyalaka *smiles and says, "I wondered when you would ask that question." She explains:*

When the door opens, an opportunity, color, emotion, or idea comes into your life. Then the door closes, so that you can exist outside time and space in which to explore this new atmosphere of totality.

You are the clay pot - and you are the soil inside that pot - and you are the seed that sprouts out of that soil. When spirit, soul, and mind come together as the plant that receives the necessary sun, water, and love (attention), you will birth your dream.

Mya: *How does the cat enter into the picture?*

Kyalaka: *The cat is hungry. The cat reminds you that you have a body to feed while your mind, spirit, and soul are having their way with you. The cat understands nothing but that he HAS to eat. Have you ever noticed that a cat will listen to no explanation as to why his food dish is not full? Just as a baby cries until he is full? When the cat eats, he usually then relaxes, even goes to sleep to dream - the crisis is over.*

Mya: How do you know when it's time to manifest the dream in physical reality. (Hummingbird shows itself at my window).

Kyalaka: *The seed will sprout in the clay pot, and the space outside time will give birth. When the seed is born, it will cry for food, and it will want to love and be loved. Then and only then will it be transported to that physical realm in the universe where it can experience, where it can root, where it* can feel "THE MOTHER." It brings with it timelessness frozen, unlimited love tested, and spirit with feet of clay.

This new dream will be squeezed out like a fetish in a pot. You will see your dream on earth, and that dream will lift its feathery body into the cavity called the heart. From there it will sing its song and paint its masterpiece. From there it will change the heartbeat of "THE MOTHER"; it will soothe her birth pangs and make her proud and elated beyond description.

Sheweia, you are the mother AND the child. You bring the idea that people are what they create. "You create your reality" is true but only part of the picture. Your reality in turn creates you. That which you love loves you back. No unrequited love here - a love that transcends and DREAMS.

I AM the Angel of Crystal Rainbows

I AM
THE ANGEL OF CRYSTAL RAINBOWS, AND ELEPHANT
MEMORIES AND MOTHER/CHILD RELATIONSHIPS.
I AM THE SILKEN GOWN OF WHISPERS AND COOS, OF BREEZES
THAT SEEM TO CARE, OF SWEETNESS THAT IS PURE. I COME
ONLY TO DELIGHT AND TO UPLIFT AND INSPIRE. I HAVE MANY
FACES, BUT ONLY ONE HEART - THE SACRED FEMININE.

162

AFTERWORD

Writing this book has been like following the bread crumbs on the path home. I was never given sight of a long stretch of the path at a time because my psyche couldn't have tolerated it, and when I was given revelation and painful truths, my awareness faded to make way for the demands of day to day living and loving. Even though recognized, these "insights" were not on the surface. In other words, they were jewels at the bottom of the sea. How could suffering be a jewel? The suffering came, not from the truth itself, but when I could not accept the <u>implications</u> <u>of the truth</u>, and I abandoned myself to keep the "expected" story in place.

It was like trying to push universes into one grain of sand. I deposited reams of confusion, searching, and pain onto one page at a time. Later, the pages revealed insights into the fabric of the story and "the knowing" all along.

In a meditation years ago, I experienced a Mother's search for her long lost daughter as my own. I repeatedly cried out her name, "Ishika!" The name haunted me over the years, bringing such emotion and tenderness and yearning.

In 2013, I put the name in the computer browser, hoping for a lead. I did find it in a list of possible girl names for parents to name their babies. ISHIKA WAS THERE! It was real and it had a history. Astounded, I read - a Sanskrit word - meaning "a sacred pen, a... painter's brush." Continuing to search - I found the full circle to my journey. The word Ishika, for the Indian culture, means "LOVE."

www.artbysheweia111.com

BIBLIOGRAPHY

Andrews, Lynn V. Crystal Woman: The Sisters of the Dreamtime. New York, NY: Warner, 1988. Print.

Bianco, Margery Williams, and Michael Hague. *The Velveteen Rabbit, Or, How Toys Become Real.* New York: Holt, Rinehart and Winston, 1983. Print.

Carey, Ken. *Return of the Bird Tribes.* San Francisco, Calif.: Harper San Francisco, 1991. Print.

Carson David, Sams, Jamie. Dragonfly #27. Medicine Cards: The discovery of Power Through the Ways of Animals. Santa Fe, N>M>, Bear & Company, 1988. p. 144-145.

Gardner, Helen; Dela Croix, Horst; Tansey, Richard G. Art Through the Ages. (II Renaissance and Modern Art) San Diego: Harcourt Brace Jovanovich, 1991. p. 650.

Hanson, Lawrence, and Elizabeth Hanson. "147." The Seekers: Gauguin, Van Gogh, Cezanne. New York: Random House, 1963. Print.

Herbert, Frank. Chapterhouse, Dune. New York: Putnam, 1985. Print.

Holger, Kalweit. *Shamans, healers, and medicine men.* Boston: Shambhala, 1991. p. 4.

Jordan, June. "we are the ones we have been waiting for" Poem for South African Women from Passion (1980) Web. >http://www.junejordan.net/poem-for-south-african-women.html.

Lord Byron. *She Walks in Beauty. Poetry Foundation. Web. <http:www.poetryfoundation.org/ poem/173100>*

Paladin, David Chethlahe. Painting the Dream: The Visionary Art of Navajo Painter David Chethlahe Paladin. Rochester, VT: Park Street, 1992. Print., p. 25, 62.

Seth, Jane Roberts, and Robert F. Butts. *Seth Speaks: The Eternal Validity of the Soul.* San Rafael, CA: New World Library, 1994. Print.

"THE EPIC STORY OF HOW HUMANS MADE ART, AND ART MADE US HUMAN." PBS. PBS, 2006.

Web: 11 Apr: 2014. <http://www.pbs.org/howartmadetheworld/>

Van Gogh, Vincent. *The Complete Letters of Vincent van Gogh with reproductions of all the drawings in the correspondences (Volume I, II, and III).* Boston [u.a] & Bulfinch Press [u.a]. 2000.